DESIRE AND PROTECT

BOOK FIVE IN THE HEROES OF EVERS, TEXAS SERIES

LORI RYAN

OTHER BOOKS BY LORI RYAN

The Sutton Billionaires Series:

The Billionaire Deal

Reuniting with the Billionaire

The Billionaire Op

The Billionaire's Rock Star

The Billionaire's Navy SEAL

Falling for the Billionaire's Daughter

The Sutton Capital Intrigue Series:

Cutthroat

Cut and Run

Cut to the Chase

The Sutton Capital on the Line Series:

Pure Vengeance

Latent Danger

The Triple Play Curse Novellas:

Game Changer

Game Maker

Game Clincher

The Heroes of Evers, TX Series:

Love and Protect

Promise and Protect

Honor and Protect (An Evers, TX Novella)

Serve and Protect

Desire and Protect

Cherish and Protect

Treasure and Protect

The Dark Falls, CO Series:

Dark Falls

Dark Burning

Dark Prison

Coming Soon – The Halo Security Series:

Dulce's Defender

Hannah's Hero

Shay's Shelter

Callie's Cover

Grace's Guardian

Sophie's Sentry

Sienna's Sentinal

For the most current list of Lori's books, visit her website: loriryanromance.com.

1

Embrace life. Always.

— Fiona O'Malley's Journal

This was going poorly. Then again, what had she expected? Phoebe Joy had given a lot of thought to the town she wanted to settle in, but not a single thought in the world to whether there would be a job for her there when she did.

So, here she was, applying for a job as a paralegal. This was the new Phoebe Joy.

She'd gotten her degree in paralegal studies years before to appease her father, but she hadn't ever used it. She'd dusted off that bad boy and hit the wanted ads with a vengeance. And now, armed with said paralegal degree and really very little else, she sat in the law office of Shane J. Bishop, Attorney-at-Law, trying not to squirm in her seat as the suited man read her résumé.

She was forcing herself to ignore the fact that he didn't look at all like she'd thought he would. When she thought small town lawyer, she thought of white hair and wire rimmed glasses. Or a large belly that said he spent too much time sitting in front of a computer. This man, well, he had none of that. He was tall, dark, and troubling. Troubling because the tall and dark part was all put together too damned well. Dark hair, dark eyes, chiseled jaw.

Phoebe shook her head to clear the thoughts and reminded herself she was supposed to be ignoring all of that.

He glanced up at her, scowled, then looked back at her résumé.

Just as she thought. No one was going to take her seriously. Her name had set her up for that years ago. Who names a baby Phoebe Joy? If your last name is Joy, your parents really should come up with a very serious name to go with it, like Susan or Jill.

Phoebe frowned. Jill doesn't work. Jill Joy is no good. Jane doesn't work either. Susan isn't horrible. Susan Joy. That could work. Suzanne might be even better.

But, Phoebe Joy. That had set her up. No one can take anyone named Phoebe Joy seriously. There was a time when she'd have liked that. She hadn't wanted to be taken overly seriously. But things were different now.

Her dad could have changed it at any point after her mom had left. Someday, she'd need to ask why he hadn't. His last name was Brophy. Why hadn't he changed her name to Phoebe Brophy? She supposed she could have done the same at some point in the eleven years since she'd turned eighteen.

Or better, she could have gone back to the original French spelling of the name: Joie. That would have worked. Not that she knew anything about her mother's ancestry or the family name. Or the entire family, for that matter. She'd simply looked it up on ancestry.com one day.

"So, uh, Ms. Joy. It looks like you've had several jobs since you received your degree, none of which have been in any way related to paralegal studies." He did have a way of putting rather a fine point on things, didn't he? She glued her bottom to the seat and refused to squirm.

"Is that a question?" *Oh crap. That's probably not a good way to start an interview.* She tried again. "I mean, no. I haven't used my paralegal degree yet. I've been doing other things." *Brilliant. Just brilliant, Phoebe.*

"Yes, I can see that. You spent a year scooping ice cream at Ben's Old-Fashioned Scoops, two years as a receptionist at Ray's Tattoo and Piercing Pagoda, two years at a paint-your-own pottery studio, and..." He glanced up at her briefly before lowering his eyes to the page again. "A month? A month at a pet store cleaning out the animal cages?"

"I've included references from all of them," Phoebe smiled, wondering briefly why on earth she'd put the one month stint at the pet store on there. How do you explain to someone that you've spent several years of your adult life being a free spirit, only to realize that's not what you want? What you want is stability, a home, a family, a decent steadfast man to come home to? Like the one sitting in front of her.

Shut up, Phoebe.

"Yes," he nodded, "I can see that. Excellent references from all of them, in fact. They all have wonderful things to say about you. Including Ray, the tattoo artist who 'hopes you'll come back to him someday and make an honest man of him'."

Was it her imagination or did Shane Bishop just flinch at the exact moment that she had? Can you call jinx on a flinch? Because if you could, maybe she could get a free soda out of this interview at the very least.

She'd spent several years hiking and traveling. She'd thought about putting that on her résumé, but hiking the Appalachian Trail and living off your dad while you found yourself wasn't really anything to recommend her, was it? She'd been happy with her vagabond ways. Her dad, on the other hand, well...he'd had higher aspirations in mind. She and her father had finally come up with a deal. She'd get her paralegal degree and then she could either choose to use it or not. She chose not. Until now.

She wondered if she should simply end the interview before things went any further down the proverbial hill. No. That wasn't like her. She might be considered flighty by many people, but she wasn't a quitter. Well, the pet store... she'd quit that. But that was because she'd been about to be fired. When your boss caught you trying to let all twelve of the store's tortoises slip out the door to freedom, you had very little say in the matter. It was quit or be fired.

As it turned out, her boss had been tempted to do the same himself. He'd been almost apologetic in telling her she was going to be fired if she didn't leave on her own. It was why he continued giving her glowing recommendations despite the incident.

The other references had all been earned the honest way. She'd made herself indispensable. It was one of the things her dad had drilled into her. You work hard, take initiative, and make yourself indispensable, so that if you ever leave, it's your own choice. And if you ever need a raise, he'd say with a laugh, that's your own choice, too.

Phoebe raised her chin and plowed forward. "I wanted to spend some time gaining experience before putting my paralegal degree to work. I traveled some, worked with a wide range of people, and—" she gestured toward the résumé "—gained valuable management and customer relations experience at each of the positions I held."

She mentally crossed her fingers behind her back. She hadn't attained anything of the sort at the pet store. It was the one exception.

She hoped he couldn't see through her. The truth was she had been floating for the last few years. Of course, she hadn't realized it at the time. As it turned out, she wasn't always the most aware person in the world. Take, for example, her latest relationship.

She'd spent eighteen months with Michael Williams. Eighteen months where she thought they were building something, heading somewhere. It had taken a single afternoon at a friend's wedding to nip that fantasy in the bud.

Shane Bishop stared at the woman in front of him. She wore

a black pantsuit with the smallest hint of a bright purple blouse beneath it. She didn't need to wear a suit to the office any more than he did. He should really consider dressing down on days he didn't need to go to court. Her hair looked as if it would like to wrestle itself out of the pins and ties she'd used to put it back in a twist. Blonde curls peeked out at the edges of her heart-shaped face and he had the bizarre urge to tell her she didn't need to wear it pinned up, either.

The truth was, she could pretty much dictate her terms. Her salary, hours, and wardrobe were all open to negotiation. What wasn't open to negotiation was whether he would hire her. Despite the fact that her résumé offered a strange hodge-podge of experience, none of which was related to the law, she was the most qualified applicant he'd had since his last paralegal had left town six months ago.

Evers, Texas, was a small place. It might be growing dramatically, but it still wasn't a big city. There was a growing artist population, but you had to drive thirty minutes to get to a movie theater and there weren't any concerts or anything bigger than small local theater productions.

A lot of people didn't want to stay. He needed to make sure she did. He'd had only two other applicants; Mrs. Steinecker, who could no longer hear but refused to get a hearing aid, and a man who wanted to know if it would be acceptable to be nude around the office, provided they didn't have any clients coming in that day.

"How soon would you be able to start?" he asked. The shock on her face when she turned back to him was amusing, but Shane kept the humor from showing on his face.

"Um, Monday? I could begin Monday, if you'd like," she said, confusion making her eyebrows knit together and the cupid bow of her lips purse up.

Distraction. That was the one thing he thought of when he looked at Phoebe Joy. She was going to be a distraction. On the other hand, maybe she'd be able to help him get caught up. He looked at the work piled in his inbox. It seemed like the pile hadn't gotten any smaller in recent months.

He looked back to Ms. Joy with a nod. "Good. I'll see you Monday, then."

"Oh." She said this with a bit of shock and he found himself fighting a smile for the second time. If nothing else, she'd entertain him. Lord, he hoped she did more than that, though. He needed someone competent.

They tied up the details and she walked out.

Shane walked to the low chest of filing cabinets that fronted his window and began flicking through the files he'd stacked there. A flash of pink—well, what he thought of as pink but had once been informed was peach—caught his eye out the window. Mindy Mason waved at him as she crossed the lawn to the library. He raised his hand in a wave but didn't smile. If he was too friendly, he'd learned, she would come over to talk and he'd never be rid of her.

Mindy Mason was one of what he thought of in his head as the Sweater Sets. He frowned to himself as he looked back down at the folder. There were three of them in town and there was a time he'd thought he'd marry one of the Sweater Sets. Unfortunately, it turned out, they'd all bored him to tears.

"Sweater sets. So damned tired of peach sweater sets," Shane mumbled under his breath. He didn't hear the door to his office open. "Why are they always peach, anyway?" He thought of the bright purple blouse hiding under Phoebe Joy's suit, but shoved the thought aside right away. Not only was she not the right kind of woman for him, she was his employee. Or she would be on Monday, anyway.

The Sweater Sets were supposed to be the right kind of woman for him. He grimaced.

"Why are what always peach?" Cade's voice came right behind him, causing Shane to jump a foot, which had to have been Cade's intention.

"Funny, little brother." Shane grabbed a stack of papers from a nearby table and sat at his desk. If he looked busy enough, he could get Cade out of there and get back to figuring out what it was about Phoebe Joy that had gotten under his skin. "My new paralegal doesn't start until Monday and I've got a pile of work to get through. Did you need something?"

"Wow. Sorry. Moody, huh? You want me to have Mama run some Midol and an apple pie or something over for you?" Cade asked, kicking his feet up onto the desk and ignoring the look Shane sent his way. Cade might be the more laid back of the two brothers, but he did like egging Shane on.

Shane just glared at him. He'd found staying quiet when Cade was in one of these moods was usually his best bet. In fact, it was the best way to flip the situation and irritate Cade.

"Oh, wow, was it the beautiful woman who just left your office that has you all in a snit?" Cade asked.

Apparently, no strategy was going to stop Cade today.

"That beautiful woman—happily-married brother of mine—is my new paralegal."

"Very happily married, you might add. Doesn't mean I don't take note when a beautiful woman gets my brother's boxers all in a bunch," Cade said, an all-too-smug grin firmly planted on his face. "Well, I'll tell Ma you'll be making it to Sunday dinners again now that you've finally hired someone to help you here. That's actually the reason I'm here. She sent me to tell you if you didn't make it this Sunday, she'd skin you and serve you for next week's dinner. I thought that was pretty gross, but I wasn't about to argue with her. She's been in a bad mood since you started missing dinners three months back."

Shane grunted. He wouldn't be any more caught up on Sunday than he was now, but at least he'd have help starting Monday. Just what kind of help that would be, he had no idea. He caught himself looking at the door again, thinking about the woman who'd just left. Hiring her might have been a big mistake. What little help she'd probably be with no experience in law couldn't possibly make up for the enormous distraction she was. Shane pulled his eyes away and refocused on Cade—who was still grinning like a damn Cheshire cat.

"What?" Shane demanded.

Cade laughed and shook his head. "Oh, nothing, Big Brother. Nothing at all."

2

Joy is worth reaching for.

— FIONA O'MALLEY'S JOURNAL

*A*nd, she's dancing

Not just dancing. She was on top of a chair, reaching up to stack books on a shelf, shaking her butt in a way that had Shane rooted to the spot in her office doorway. This was his new paralegal. Sure, he hadn't expected her to be here this early, and it was a positive that she was, but he also didn't expect her to have *Low Rider* playing as she ... did whatever it was she was doing. The present move included raising her hands above her head and doing a little swivel, twisty thing. When the chair moved under her, she squealed and caught herself on the shelf, before starting up again.

Also unexpected? His reaction to the wiggling hips in front of him. He should be annoyed. Shane swallowed hard, torn between casually announcing his presence, hauling her off the chair before she fell, and grabbing her and finding out what it would feel like to have his hands on—

So not going there. Not with someone who worked for him. Someone he needed to keep working for him. And, someone who was so clearly not the type of woman he usually chose, the type of woman he needed in his life.

The next few seconds happened in slow motion. At least, he was fairly sure they did. She turned on the chair, right in the middle of the "take a little trip" line and let out a scream. Well, maybe it was more a yelp. Halfway between a yelp and a scream.

And then the chair wobbled and seemed to spin a bit to the left as Phoebe corrected with her body to the right. And then she was flying.

Not exactly flying.

Falling.

Hard.

Shane bolted forward, trying to catch her but failing. He got to her seconds after she fell.

"Phoebe!" His head was running through the worker's compensation insurance plan he had as he all but skidded to her side on his knees. "Are you all right? Phoebe?"

She turned over, pulling her hair out of her face with one hand and his heart stopped in his chest. She was laughing. Laughing without embarrassment or hesitation or anything. No worry that he'd seen her dancing on her chair. No concern for her safety or anything like that. Just pure, well...joy.

And it was stunning. She was gorgeous when she wasn't trying to impress at a job interview or worry about what he might think.

Damn. Shane had a problem. A big one. And now, that problem was all but sprawled in his lap in a heap.

3

Small moments of joy can build a lifetime of happiness.

— FIONA O'MALLEY'S JOURNAL

Phoebe straightened her skirt and sat in the chair Shane had now pulled around to the back of her desk. She'd turned off the music and tried to look like she belonged in a law firm, but she wasn't completely sure he was buying it. If the stony look on his face meant anything, he wasn't.

"Sorry about that. I thought I was the only one in here this early." She pulled her hair back in a ponytail and quickly clipped it with the large butterfly clip she'd left on her desk earlier. It wouldn't hold for long, but it should make her a little more presentable while he was in the room.

He waved a hand in dismissal and sat in the chair opposite her desk. "Margaret won't be in until nine and I don't schedule appointments until then, but I come in early most days."

"I'll remember that." She pressed her lips together.

"Well, as long as we're both here," he said, "We can get you started on some assignments. Margaret will get you the tax forms and things you'll need to sign when she comes in later."

He stood and gestured for her to follow him, and she couldn't help but notice he was in khaki pants and a pullover shirt this morning. He led the way to his office and gestured for her to take a seat.

"I always thought Fridays were supposed to be business casual. You had a suit on Friday but casual today?" She made the comment without thinking and then realized it could be considered rude.

He apparently didn't think so because he offered a shrug as he looked over his shoulder at her. "I've decided that on days I'm not going into the courthouse, I'll dress business casual. You're welcome to as well, if you'd like."

Phoebe nodded, but on the inside, she was breathing a huge sigh of relief. She only had two suits. The black skirt-suit she was wearing today, and a navy pantsuit, which was also the suit she'd worn for her interview. Relocating from Austin had cost her a small chunk of her savings, and then there had been the deposit on the duplex she was renting three blocks from her office. She planned to pair different blouses with the two suits for at least a month or two until she got a few paychecks stocked away and caught up on her expenses.

If she could do business casual, she had a few skirts in

her closet that she could pair with the blouses instead. With sandals, they would do well and she could save her suits for any days she needed to go to court with Shane. Assuming, he would ever need her to go to court with him. She wasn't really sure what he would want.

She realized he wasn't one for wasted words. Unlike her. She'd need to keep her lips pressed together around him. She tended to babble, always wanting to fill empty silences. But that was one of the things she planned to change about herself.

Not that it would be easy, what with all the silences he was leaving. Good heavens, did the man never talk?

"I love this old building. It's gorgeous." So much for keeping her mouth shut. She looked around at the high ceiling that matched the one in her office. "I wonder what era it's from?"

Now he spoke, startling her out of her study of the pressed tin tile ceilings that had been painted a distressed white. Or maybe they hadn't been painted that way. Maybe they were actually distressed. "I'm told it's an old rancher's weekend cottage. I should research it more, I guess, but—" He didn't finish the sentence. He simply looked around at the work piled up on his desk and the filing cabinet behind him.

She supposed she should dig in and help him with that work, but she had to admit, she was curious about the building. "Ranchers had weekend cottages in town?"

"Mm hmm." He pulled the stack of files in front of them and began sorting a few from the rest. "In the early 1900s, I guess. They would keep very small cottages like this one in town to visit on the weekends. One of my clients told me she thought the ceiling tiles were not original. I would guess she's right." He shrugged, looking up at the ceiling. "Well, she knew better than I would anyway."

"You wouldn't think the ceilings would be so high down here. It's such a small house, there's barely room for the second floor."

"There's not." Shane leaned back in his chair and looked around. "The upstairs is basically one open bedroom with a window on either side. It's almost more of an attic. I use it for storage. I have to bend over when I go up there."

"How tall are you?" Phoebe's eyes went wide. "That was probably rude."

He looked at her, stunned for a minute, before laughing. "Six-two."

Phoebe nodded, looking again at the ceiling hoping to hide the fact that she was thinking about that height and how nice it was. She wasn't quite sure when it happened—maybe back when she'd noticed his khaki pants, which she'd of course been viewing from the back—but she seemed to have become a little too aware of Shane's not very lawyerly body. She wondered how he kept so fit when, according to him, he spent almost every minute in the office trying to catch up on work.

Shane cleared his throat and Phoebe looked back to him, her cheeks heating. "Sorry. You probably want to get started on work." She scooted forward to the edge of her chair, ready to look over the files he was now pushing toward her.

"Take a look through these. I tried to pull out things that

I was sure you'd have gone over in school. Simple things like title searches, preparing a deed transfer, that kind of thing."

Phoebe pulled the files toward her and started flipping through them, nodding her head.

"If you don't know how to do something, just ask me. I'll typically have a pile of things for you to start on each morning, and I'll leave another pile with Margaret throughout the day. If you check with her after lunch, she'll have more things for you."

"And should I just give her anything I've completed? Or would you rather I bring them straight to you?" Phoebe realize she was feeling nervous, not something she typically felt when she started a new job. Then again, this wasn't like the other jobs she had.

"You can give them to Margaret."

With that, he looked down at his own pile of folders and Phoebe was left with the distinct feeling she was dismissed.

She closed the folders in her lap and scooted out of the office, wishing she could dismiss the thoughts in her head as easily as Shane had dismissed her. For whatever reason, just being around Shane Bishop made her stomach jumpy.

4

You've got to do your own growing, no matter how tall your father was.

— Irish Proverb Recorded in Fiona O'Malley's
Journal

Shane stuck his head out of his office. "Anything I need to look at, Margaret?"

Margaret had been screening his emails for him for the better part of a year. It was one of the ways they'd ended up managing without a paralegal for so long.

"I flagged three things for you to look at." She spun around in her desk chair to face him. "Oh, and Phoebe left these for you before she went to lunch."

Shane stepped closer and took the files from Margaret. It seemed to be all the files Shane had given Phoebe that morning. He frowned down at them. "She's finished already?" The comment was said absently, not really needing an answer. Margaret didn't give him one.

He scanned through everything and was surprised to find everything was in order. Not only had she finished what he asked of her, she left sticky notes with little comments here and there throughout the pages. Suggestions or things he needed to be aware of.

Sticky notes with little comments and smiley faces.

He glanced up at Margaret, realizing he'd need to come up with more work for Phoebe. Thank God. "Would you mind calling over to Gina and asking her if she can get something ready for me? I'll run out and pick it up in a little bit." Gina and her sister, Tina, owned the Two Sisters Diner and provided most of Shane's lunches.

"No need. Phoebe asked if she could pick us up anything. I brought my lunch today, but I'm having her get you something." She looked at her watch. "She should be back in about 10 minutes."

Shane looked back to his office then around to Margaret again. "You know, I think I'll walk over and meet her. I could use the break." There was a time he never missed getting out for a run at lunch or walking over to eat with friends. If he was finally going to be breaking the chains that had bound him to his desk lately, he should start taking advantage of that freedom.

The walk to the diner wasn't far. Shane raised a hand in response to waves from several people across the street or passing by in cars. He spotted Phoebe when he was half a block away coming out of the diner. He hadn't realized how much gold was in her hair, but with the sun shining off its strands, it was hard to miss.

And where the hell had that thought come from?

Her forehead creased when she reached him. "I'm sorry. Am I late getting back?" Her tone said she hadn't thought she was and he shook his head, smiling at her.

"Not at all. I just figured I'd get out of the office and walk you back. Is that for me?" He pointed to the brown paper bag in her hands.

She turned it over to him. "Yes. Margaret said to tell them to make you your usual, so that's what I did. Let's hope they got it right."

"In the diner, make me my usual is code for surprise me." He opened the bag and sniffed before letting out a moan. "Meatloaf sandwich. You haven't lived until you've had the meatloaf sandwich at the diner made from Tina's leftover meatloaf. Sunday, the special is always meatloaf but she doubles up and makes enough to have meatloaf sandwiches for the special on Mondays."

Shane gestured to a side street on the right. "Let's go this way. I'll show you some of the town."

They wandered through several side streets, with Shane pointing out various things for her. He pointed to the elementary school, which was also across from the building that housed both the middle and high schools.

"Wow. You can fit the middle and high school classes into one building?"

"Oh yeah. They might have to split that sometime in the next few years, but while I was growing up, we were lucky if there were three or four hundred students total in the building. It's a small town." He looked around. "Well, I take that back. It's a small town that's growing bigger. For a while the economy was pretty depressed, but we've made a comeback recently. I think the building now holds six hundred, but last I heard they were at capacity."

Shane stopped, turning to a small house. He could feel Phoebe's eyes bouncing from him to the yard and back as he greeted the short round woman kneeling by a garden patch at the front of the lawn. "Well this one is interesting, Isabel. I never thought... Well I just never... Well, it's interesting."

Isabel shaded her eyes as she looked up at him, beaming herself. "I have to say, I wasn't sure about this one when I started, but I think it's come out nicely."

Said garden plot was well-tended with freshly tilled soil and no evidence of a weed or errant plant in sight. In fact, there were no plants. Rubber chickens stuck out of the soil in neat little rows, as if they'd been planted there and grown as flowers.

"Isabel Schneider meet my new paralegal, Phoebe Joy. Phoebe, this is Isabel." Shane glanced at Phoebe expecting to see a dropped jaw, but what he saw was a friendly and accepting smile. Not many people pulled that off when they first ran into Isabel's garden.

"It's a pleasure to meet you, Ms. Schneider." Phoebe extended her hand and Isabel stood, brushing off the dirt on a pair of navy blue khakis before accepting the handshake.

"Likewise."

The small group turned as an old truck pulled into the driveway next to Isabel's. A white-haired man leaned out the window and scowled in their direction.

"Are you kidding me? You have to be kidding me. Chickens?" Now he looked Shane directly in the eye. "Do something about this. There are rubber chickens in the ground."

Shane raised his hands. "Not getting involved." With a smile toward Phoebe, he steered them down the street as the neighbors continued bickering.

Phoebe leaned toward him, their arms brushing. "Please tell me you're going to explain that."

He liked the proximity. "About three years back, Isabel and her brother had a falling out. She started planting unusual things in her garden. Actually, it wasn't all that unusual at first. They were flowers, at least. Plastic ones, but flowers. She still occasionally does plastic flowers, but more often than not it's something like pinwheels or flags. Rubber chickens is a whole new level." He looked back at the dueling neighbors and shook his head.

"Wait, that's her brother?" Phoebe's eyes went wide and Shane laughed at the look she gave him.

"Yep. She swears the garden is to entertain her grandchildren, but since the youngest of them just turned 12, that excuse always seems a little flimsy in my mind."

"You think she's doing it just to get her brother?"

"Oh yeah." Shane raised his hand in greeting to another passing car as they turned back toward the office.

"You know everybody, don't you." Phoebe's gaze followed the car before returning to him.

Shane lifted his shoulder. "I grew up here. I'm also the only lawyer in town. I handle almost all the real estate transactions, unless it's somebody buying from out of town and they use a lawyer from back home. I handle a lot of the litigation."

"I noticed trust and estate matters seem to make up a lot of your workload. I mean, if what you gave me this morning was any indication."

He didn't have a chance to answer her. They'd circled back around to the law office and chief Garret Hensley was approaching the front steps of the building from the other side. Something about the man's gaze told Shane this wasn't a friendly visit, despite the fact the two men were friends.

"Garret? Everything all right?" Shane asked when they got close enough.

The chief removed his hat. "I'm sorry, Shane. I just need a word in private."

"All right. We can go in my office. Oh, Garret Hensley, chief of police, meet my new paralegal, Phoebe Joy. Phoebe this is our chief, Garret Hensley."

The three moved into the front entrance and stopped in the lobby of the office. Margaret must have stepped out to eat her lunch at the park because she was nowhere in sight.

"It's nice to meet you, chief." Phoebe said with a nod. "I think I met your wife at lunch. Ashley?"

As always, the mention of Ashley brought a relaxed smile to the Chief's face. "That's right. She's usually one of the first people you meet when you get to town. She's pretty fond of taking people under her wing and showing them around."

"She introduced me to Katelyn and Laura, and just about everybody in the diner." Phoebe looked from Shane to the chief and then gestured over her shoulder to her office. "I'll leave you two alone. Shane, is it all right if I poke around in some of the computer files to get a sense of how you like some of your documents set up and formatted?"

"Absolutely. I'll get you some more work as soon as Garret and I have finished."

Once Shane had shut the door to his office, Garret let out a breath. "I'm sorry, Shane. I hate to have to tell you this, but Fiona O'Malley was found dead in her home this morning."

Shane sank into his chair. His neighbor wasn't the oldest woman on the planet, but she was hardly young. If memory served, she was in her late 70s. He had lived next to her for the last of those seven decades and he'd liked the woman a lot. She still spoke with the Irish lilt of her childhood and was always frank and cheerful.

He looked up at Garret. "How?"

"That's what I'm hoping to talk to you about. I'm not here to talk to you in your capacity as her lawyer. I understand you have confidentiality issues to worry about there. I'm interested in talking to you as her neighbor, her friend."

Shane nodded. Garret would never ask Shane to violate attorney-client privilege.

"It appears to be suicide. I just wanted to get your sense of things before I go talk to the daughter."

"Her daughter lives over in Blanco I think."

Garret nodded. "I'll drive over there this afternoon. The medical examiner won't formalize anything yet, but it looks like she might have overdosed intentionally. Her blood pressure medication. We found a bottle next to her and it was empty."

Shane shook his head, not wanting to believe Fiona would take her own life. "Why?" He didn't really mean to ask the question of Garret. It was just what came out.

"I don't know. I was hoping you could help me with that."

"Who found her?" Shane rubbed a hand down his face. Fiona was in a very happy relationship. He thought so, anyway. She and her boyfriend lived together, and despite their age difference, they seemed committed. He hoped Elliot wasn't the one to find her. It would crush the man.

"Beverly Newman found her. She said they were supposed to have lunch together." Beverly was Fiona's neighbor on the other side, and also her best friend. "When Mrs. O'Malley didn't come over, she went to check on her. She let herself in with her key and found her in bed."

"Does Elliot know?" There was no need to ask if Garret knew Fiona well enough to know who Elliot was. Aside from the fact that Garret knew many of the people in town even after only being the chief of police for a year, there probably wasn't anyone in town who didn't know about Fiona and Elliot. At least not anyone who'd lived there for any amount of time.

Elliot was in his early forties. To say the couple had garnered some attention when they started dating was the understatement of the century. It had been a scandal that kept the rumor mill of Evers chugging right along for months. And when Elliot had moved in, the scandal had been renewed.

Anyone who knew them, though, usually saw the love between the two. Shane had.

"Yes. He offered to go tell her daughter, but I have a feeling that would be a bad idea. They don't exactly get along and he's pretty wrecked. I don't think making the drive right now would be very safe."

Shane sat in stunned silence for a few minutes. "You said you needed to talk to me as her friend and neighbor. What can I do?"

"Like I said, the medical examiner won't be able to finalize his determination of suicide immediately. I was just hoping you might have some insight into her state of mind lately. Her daughter will have questions."

Shane didn't envy this part of the job for Garret. Hell, he didn't envy any part of the job for Garret. "She seemed happy. At least I thought so. I haven't seen her as often lately as I used to because of my workload, but for the most part she was happy. She and Elliot seemed to be, anyway." He rubbed at the back of his neck and tilted his head. "She'd had some...issues, but I didn't think it would lead to anything like this."

Garret sat forward, but didn't comment. He was always one to just wait and see what was going to come out. It was a tactic Shane recognized and used himself.

"Memory issues, confusion. That sort of thing." Shane had to be careful because he was now skirting the line of attorney-client privilege and that privilege wasn't something that went away with the client's death.

Fiona O'Malley had come to see him as a client when that confusion began, but she'd also talked to him about it as a friend at home first. He couldn't discuss what they'd talked about in his office, but their discussions as friends weren't off limits.

"Alzheimer's?" Garret asked.

"I don't know that she actually went in for any diagnosis, but I know she was worried about some type of dementia. Her brother lived for years with severe dementia. She had to watch him suffer for a long time. She knows—knew—the strain it put on the whole family."

Garret let out a breath. "So, would it surprise you if we find she took her own life to avoid that?"

Shane shook his head. "No, but I didn't think things had gone so far that she might do that. I know she worried about Elliot, though. She didn't want to put him through what her sister-in-law went through with her brother."

"Anything else you can tell me?"

"No. Not that I can think of." And not that he could share. Fiona had asked him to empty her safe-deposit box when she died and deliver the contents to various people when he took care of her estate. He had prepared her will for her several years back and she'd updated it recently. He couldn't share any of those details with Garret unless Garret opened an investigation and obtained a court order.

The two men stood and Garret reached across the desk to pump Shane's hand once more. "Thanks, Shane. I still can't give her daughter any definitive answers just yet, but I'll at least be able to tell her what we think might have been going on with her mother."

5

There are times when embracing life is harder than one would think. Friends, it seems, make all the difference.

— Fiona O'Malley's Journal

P hoebe sat at the back of the church. Shane had invited her to sit in front with him, but she hadn't felt right doing that. She was only here as a mark of respect for a woman the whole town seemed to adore. Shane gave a eulogy that was marked with love and the humor she'd heard Fiona O'Malley had always filled her life with.

Phoebe had heard a great deal about Fiona O'Malley in the last few days, and she'd been left with the sense she would have liked the woman very much. Fiona didn't seem to put much stock in what other people thought about her. She sounded like a woman who put family, friends, and joy above all else.

Although, this morning Phoebe had noticed some whisperings about Fiona and her daughter not getting along so well in recent years. Her daughter sat in the front row now, her husband by her side, and two small children tucked in next to her. Phoebe guessed they might be five and seven.

The congregation stood, ready to file out and head to the cemetery for the burial. Phoebe kept her head ducked and slipped out of the church and off to the side. She planned to wait for Shane to let him know she wouldn't be going to the burial. She would get the office open and catch up on some of the work they needed to get done. With Fiona's death this week, Shane had taken one afternoon and the following morning off, something she knew he didn't do very often. She might have only been in town the week, but if one thing was clear, it was that Shane Bishop worked far too much.

Another thing had become clear in the last few days. Shane Bishop was something of, if not a patriarch, then at least a brother to the town. He seemed to not only know everyone, but care deeply about how they were and what they needed. People seemed to rely on him not only for legal work, but for other things as well. She'd seen people ask him for advice again and again. She had also seen people lean on him in the last few days as they grieved the loss of one of their own.

Watching Elliot grieve had been particularly heart-wrenching. It was clear the man loved Fiona O'Malley, and he seemed as though he might be a bit lost without her.

Shane hadn't yet emerged. Phoebe knew he would be speaking to everybody on his way out of the church, but Margaret made her way over to where Phoebe stood.

"It was nice of you to come to the service."

Phoebe glanced around at the people milling on the sidewalk and talking about who would follow whom to the cemetery and who was going in what cars. "It seems like most of the town is here."

Margaret smiled and looked around. "She was well loved."

"I'm not going to go to the burial. I was waiting to tell Shane, but I have a feeling he's going to be in there for a while." Phoebe looked down the street toward the law office. "I'm going to go get caught up on some things at the office. I know Shane said he would be coming in after the funeral today, and there are a few things I want to prepare for him. Would you let him know for me?"

"I'm sure he doesn't expect you to go in on Saturday."

"Oh, it's all right. I don't mind, and I know he was stressed he had to miss work this week, even though he felt it was the right thing to do. He wanted to be there for Elliot and be available when Fiona's family got into town."

Margaret squeezed her hand. "You're a good girl Phoebe Joy."

She said it as though she'd only just decided this, as though maybe she'd been withholding judgment. Phoebe smiled and nodded, but quickly walked down the street toward the law office, crossing first to avoid having to walk through everyone still organizing rides outside of the church.

She let herself into the office, and started up her computer, bringing up the soundtrack to *A Knight's Tale*. She hummed to *Golden Years*, the song from the scene where Count Adhemar taunts William and Jocelyn into dancing in the movie. She'd always loved *A Knight's Tale*, but lately she'd been watching it a lot. She'd started to see a lot of parallels between what she wanted for her life and what she saw in the movie.

Not just because it had the most incredible love note in the history of love notes in it. Phoebe could never listen to the lines about the pieces of William's heart or Paris being empty without Jocelyn, and not sigh and get all misty-eyed.

It wasn't just because of the love affair the movie depicted either. It was because of the way it showed the love of someone who sees that you're not perfect and accepts you anyway. The love of someone who can love you for who you are even when who you are is deeply flawed.

Anyone who sees the movie would have to admit that Jocelyn is horribly flawed. She's materialistic and one-dimensional. William loves her despite all of that. And eventually you begin to see what he sees in Jocelyn. You see that she's not really one-dimensional, but multifaceted and loving, devoted to her friends in ways you can't help but admire.

Everyone in the movie is like that. They all have something that makes them an outcast and yet they found this family together. A family they would do anything for.

Phoebe and her father were extremely close. And she'd been close to her grandmother, when she'd been alive. That was the extent of her family. What she hadn't realized until recently was that she was apparently not very close to making her own family. It's part of what she'd come to town looking for.

That sounded awful. Like she was hunting for a

husband, and that wasn't exactly what was going on. She'd come to town to find a community, to find a place she belonged, where she could build a life. She'd realized recently that she'd somehow been cultivating superficial relationships with a lot of people, when what she really wanted was something much deeper.

Phoebe shook herself out of the fog she'd been in and got to work. She wasn't really a *feel sorry for yourself* kind of person and she didn't really want to start now.

An hour later her phone rang. "Phoebe Joy."

"Phoebe? It's Shane."

Phoebe glanced at the computer screen, surprised to see how much time had passed. "Is the burial over?" She flinched. That sounded a bit gauche.

"Yes, and I need you to do me a big favor."

"Sure, anything." Phoebe smiled, realizing she meant that. She liked working for Shane and wanted to make sure he ended up wanting her to stay here.

"Fiona's daughter is anxious to get back on the road quickly."

"Oh, she's not planning to stay for a while?"

"I guess not. I thought for sure she'd want to go through her mother's things. Emmaline and Elliot don't exactly get along, not well anyway. I still thought she'd want to be part of getting her mother's things cleaned out and given to friends or donated. But apparently she's going to leave all that to Elliot."

Phoebe murmured a response and Shane continued. "I told her I'd meet her at the law office. I have some things for her that her mother asked me to get out of her safe deposit box, but I got tied up here and I can't get back there right away."

"I'm at the office. I can handle that." Duh. He had just called her at the office. He knew perfectly well where she was.

She could almost hear the smile in Shane's response. "Thank you."

She sighed. "What is it?"

"If you go in my office there are two boxes on my desk. The one on the left is for Elliot. I'll get those things to him later. The one on the right is for her, Emmaline. It's her mother's jewelry and a journal she asked me to give to her."

"No problem. I've had the front door locked since we weren't open to the public today, but I'll unlock it and watch for her."

"Thank you, Phoebe. You're a lifesaver."

He hung up and Phoebe walked to the front door just in time to see a car pull up to the curb. The thin blonde woman Phoebe had seen in church got out of the car and leaned in the window to say something to the kids in the back.

Phoebe pushed the front door open and held it as Emmaline walked up the steps. "You must be Emmaline ..." Phoebe realized she didn't know Emmaline's married name. "Fiona O'Malley's daughter," she finished awkwardly.

"Emmaline Parker," the woman murmured politely.

Polite was the operative word. There was no warmth. Although, Phoebe supposed expecting warmth from a woman who had just buried her mother might be a bit odd. Emmaline was probably still in shock. Knowing your mother had taken her own life had to be difficult, to say the least.

"Come on in. Shane has everything ready for you." Phoebe recovered and stepped in to the front lobby. "He got tied up helping someone, but he called to let me know you were coming. He said you needed to get back on the road quickly?"

Emmaline nodded but didn't comment further.

"It's all this way." Phoebe walked into Shane's office and took a quick peek into the boxes to make sure she had the right one, before pushing the right box across the desk to Emmaline. "This box is for you."

Emmaline looked into the box. She picked up the journal and examined its cover. It was a beautiful leather binding with an ornate carved design on the front. She held it in one hand as she moved the jewelry around the box, almost as though looking for something. "Is this everything?"

"As far as I know, yes. I can double check with Shane if you'd like, but he said everything for you was in the box on the right. Apparently, your mother wanted you to have that journal," she corrected herself, "to read that journal, and Shane said the box had jewelry in it, but he didn't tell me exactly what jewelry. Do you want me to check with him?"

Emmaline glanced at the other box on the table.

"I can check with Shane." Phoebe repeated the offer, not sure she should say that the other box was for Elliot.

"That's all right. If it looks like anything is missing I'll call him once we get home." She placed the journal on the desk, lifted the box and turned to step out.

Phoebe picked up the small book. "Don't you want to read this?" It was a rude question, but Phoebe had never been very good at screening those out. Besides, if someone she was close to had committed suicide, she'd want to know why. It seemed to her, it was quite possible the journal could lead to answers where that was concerned, as well.

Shouldn't Fiona's daughter want those answers?

Emmaline glanced back over her shoulder, a mask of indifference on her face, but Phoebe could see that it was only that. A mask. "You read it if you want. I don't plan on it."

6

I want to believe that I am strong enough to let love in.

— FIONA O'MALLEY'S JOURNAL

Shane didn't think he'd ever seen Elliot Godfrey look sad. Shane hadn't had the heart to abandon him and Elliot didn't seem as though he would be ready to leave the cemetery for a long time.

For as long as Shane had known him, Elliot had been the one trying to make everybody in the room laugh. In fact, Fiona told Shane she fell in love with Elliot Godfrey the first time he made her laugh, and he hadn't stopped doing it since then. She explained he had never stopped making her laugh or making her fall in love with him. She claimed she fell deeper in love with the man each day.

Shane had asked once why they hadn't gotten married. Fiona said when you got to be her age, you didn't need things like that to solidify your relationship. Your relationship was what it was and no piece of paper from the town clerk was going to make it any stronger.

Right now, Elliot looked like all the happiness had been drained from his world.

"Oh Elliot, I just... I just don't know what to say." Miriam Green approached Elliot and Shane as several of the other mourners made their way out to the cars that lined the circular drive in the cemetery.

Miriam looked almost as defeated as Elliot, sorrow lining her face as she reached for the man's hand to squeeze it. "I'm so sorry, Elliot. She was an incredible woman."

"She was, wasn't she?" Elliot said looking from Miriam to Shane and back again. "I do believe I fell in love with her the first time I set my eyes on her."

Shane smiled. "She said the same about you, you know?"

Eyes that had never quite dried up throughout the day and were now tearing again met his. "She always told me that, but I never believed her. She took some convincing, you know. She wouldn't go out with me the first three times I asked."

"We're all going to miss her down at the center." Miriam managed the senior center in town, where Fiona had spent most of her days while Elliot ran the pharmacy he owned. "She's been lighting that place up for the entire 10 years I've run it. It just won't be the same without her."

Shane put a hand on Miriam's shoulder and squeezed, wanting to steady the woman. Her hands shook as she wiped at tears and for perhaps the first time, he realized she was catching up on the age of the people who came to her center. She had to be in her late 50s or even early 60s herself. She always seemed to have such energy, though. Not today.

Shane didn't have much energy himself today. Bereavement had a way of draining everyone it touched.

"Elliot, can I give you a lift home?"

Elliot looked back at the grave. The cemetery workers had nearly finished filling it in and the man looked for all the world like he wanted to undo their work, if only for the temporary denial it would allow him. He looked at Shane. "I'm not sure I'm ready."

"That's all right. Take your time. Ashley and Beverly are taking care of everything at the house." There was a gathering for mourners at the house, but Elliot hadn't been up to being a part of organizing that. No one blamed him, and no one expected him to. The town librarian, Ashley Hensley, had taken charge and the neighbors had arranged for potluck style refreshments. "I'll wait here until you're ready to go."

Miriam moved off to her own car and Shane saw her sit in it for a few minutes as though working to compose herself before starting the car and driving away.

Shane's mother, May, approached with her friend Josh Samuels and Shane's brother, Cade, by her side. She leaned heavily on the cane she relied on after the accident that took their father's life and much of her health and mobility.

"You'll be staying with Elliot until he's ready to go?" May spoke quietly and Shane had a feeling she knew the answer, but he nodded anyway.

"We'll see you at the house, then." Cade put a hand on

May's back and led her to the car where Cade's wife, Laura waited with their daughter, Jamie May. Laura had spent most of the time during the burial service following Jamie around the cemetery as Jamie played. She was too young to understand what was happening that day.

Laura had told Shane she thought about leaving Jamie with a sitter for the day, but Fiona had often told her how much joy she got in seeing the young girl.

When they drove away, Shane and Elliot were left alone except for the two workers finishing up and the lone figure standing under a tree several yards away. Shane wasn't sure Elliot had seen him. As far as Shane knew, Aengus O'Malley and Elliot were not good friends, but he never thought they were enemies either. Perhaps O'Malley was just giving Elliot space today.

Aengus and Fiona had been divorced years before she and Elliot met. Shane didn't think the divorce had been particularly contentious, and Aengus came to town occasionally for his work. Aengus and Fiona had visited from time to time when Aengus came through.

Shane wondered now if he should approach the man and see if he was all right, but before he could make up his mind, Aengus turned and walked away.

Shane didn't mind the next forty-five minutes he spent waiting for Elliot. When Fiona's boyfriend finally did turn with a silent nod to Shane, the two walked away with the sound of quiet crying accompanying them as Elliot continued to grieve.

7

Scary things are worth doing.

— Fiona O'Malley's Journal

Phoebe knew it was silly, but she was avoiding Shane like the plague. It turned out, even though she loved her job and the town, she was already putting everything she'd found here at risk by having a stupid crush on her boss.

She had dated her bosses before. In fact, she'd probably done it one too many times and she knew where that went. When the relationship was over, so was the job. Granted, she was usually the one to leave both of those things, but she didn't want to do that in this case. She wanted to build something more here. She wanted to belong to this town as much as everyone in it seemed to belong to one another, from what she'd seen so far.

So, when Shane came to her door looking for someone

to keep him company at lunchtime, she made an excuse. "I was planning to just work through lunch today. I'm working on tagging some of the old documents in the system with different search terms that we can use when we need something. It should save time in the long run."

Shane raised a brow at her, crossing his arms and leaning against the jamb of her office door. Why did he have to look like he just stepped out of a magazine spread?

"All the more reason to go to lunch with me. You can tell me all about it. Besides, you've been working too much lately."

Phoebe couldn't have held back the snort of laughter at that if she tried. "Wow. Nice to meet you, Pot. I'm Kettle."

The smile she got in response was of the panty melting variety. As much as she enjoyed ribbing him, she needed to make a mental note not to elicit any more of those smiles.

"Come on. I'm your boss and I'm ordering you to take a lunch break."

Phoebe shook her head, but grabbed her purse and walked with him. When he held the door for her at the front of the building, the torment began. She had known it would. It always started that way, with him holding the door so the proximity of his body as she walked past him would cause her breath to catch.

Then they'd walk the two blocks to the diner together, with his arm occasionally touching her shoulder. That set off a little spin cycle in her belly that got her so flustered, she forgot to say anything until she started filling the silence with all kinds of asinine comments.

Here comes one now. "Messages from the dead shouldn't

go unread." The words slipped out before Phoebe had a chance to stop them.

Oh great. This one actually rhymed.

This caused Shane to stumble to a stop. Not that that was a surprise. "Excuse me?"

"She never came back for the journal."

Shane looked up and down the sidewalk as though searching for some explanation that would let him know what the conversation was about.

Phoebe tried to explain. "Emmaline. She never came back to get Fiona's journal, did she?"

"Oh." Shane started walking again and she fell in line beside him. "No. I thought she might too, but she never did."

"It's just not right, not reading something that your mother left for you. I would love to have something from my mom."

"Your mom died?" She had come to realize he was a very sensitive person and the softness in his voice reflected that. As much as he put on a show in trying to live up to every expectation the town might have of its one attorney, he wasn't the stodgy conservative man he tried to be.

"No," she said.

He held the door to the diner for her as they walked in. Several minutes passed while they greeted Gina and Tina and said hello to other customers while making their way back to the booth in the corner. When they sat, he looked at her as though the conversation had only stopped that second and he was waiting for her to continue.

"She left when I was young. She was interested in me long enough to have me and to put her name on the birth certificate, but not much more after that. She left me on my dad's doorstep when I was one month old and he raised me from there."

She looked up and saw Shane watching her. "I'm sorry," he said.

She waved away his apology. It's not like he had anything to do with her mother's maternal failings and truthfully, she never liked talking about the rejection with people.

"I just meant, I would have loved to have something from her. If there was something she wanted me to read, or something she wanted me to know, I would've taken the time to read it. It just seems sad that Emmaline seems so... Well, I guess she seemed so angry."

They stopped long enough to put in their order before picking up the conversation.

"Things were strained between her mom and her over the last few years. Well," he frowned, "longer than that, I guess. She was never able to accept Elliot in her mom's life the way most people had, but there was strain on the relationship before then."

"Was Fiona a widow or were she and Emmaline's dad divorced?"

"Divorced." Shane sipped the sweet tea Gina had dropped at the table for him while Phoebe doctored her coffee.

She didn't know why she'd asked. Either way, Emmaline would have reason, at least from her perspective, to resent her mother's new boyfriend. Especially a boyfriend so much younger than her mom. Elliot was maybe ten years Emmaline's senior. That had to be strange.

Shane continued. "Aengus comes around now and again. He works in agriculture equipment financing."

Phoebe laughed. "That sounds exciting."

Shane smiled at her joke. "Yeah." He shrugged. "Anyway, I think Fiona and Aengus had moved past the divorce, but I'm not sure Emmaline ever did. In fact, I think Fiona saw more of Aengus that she did of her daughter."

They sat in silence for a minute, before Shane changed the conversation away from death, divorce, and the havoc those things can bring to peoples' lives. "So, tell me about the project you were working on at the office."

Phoebe was glad for the shift in conversation. Her thoughts had strayed to the idea of mothers and daughters and that wasn't one that ever sat well with her.

"It's not much, really. I'm just going through the documents you've created in the last year and tagging them, starting with the trusts and estates docs. I can tag things like any special terms or a type of trust that you set up or even things like the number of kids or grandkids. That way, when someone needs a new estate package set up, I can use the tags to pull out documents you've created that suit the needs of the new client, then use those to set up the new document. All you'll need to do is review it and sign off."

Shane didn't say anything so Phoebe continued. "I mean, I could set up a whole bunch of sample docs for each situation and pull from those when I need to, but this is a lot less set up and accomplishes the same thing. It also means you can tag something any time you set something up that you think we might want to use again in the future. We can do it with all kinds of things. Titles, deeds, real estate transactions, leases …" Now she was babbling. Leases were real estate transactions. So were titles and deeds, for that matter.

Shane looked a little stunned. "You can tag word documents?"

Phoebe laughed. "Yes."

"I think I love you."

It was Phoebe's turn to be stunned, and it wasn't by his words. She knew he didn't mean them. It was by the way his words made her feel. By the little back handspring her heart did at them. She covered it by laughing and throwing the crumpled sugar packet she'd been fingering at him. Probably not something one was supposed to do with your boss, but it made him offer one of those grins. *The* grin. The one she loved to bring out in him.

"I'll show you how to do it when we get back to the office," she said, just as their food arrived.

They finished their meal and exited the diner. "They need more restaurants in town," Phoebe said.

Shane looked at her in mock shock that she'd dare to utter the words, but she laughed. "I'm serious. Either that, or I need to start bringing a lunch more often. If I keep eating at Tiny's and the diner, I'll need to buy a new wardrobe soon."

She'd been introduced to Tiny's Barbecue the day before with Ashley, Laura, and Katelyn, who she was quickly realizing she liked a lot. Laura was married to Shane's brother and Katelyn had married John Davies, who was the county's sheriff. The three women had welcomed her into their group as though they'd known her for years.

Shane looked like he was about to respond, but a shout cut into their conversation, causing Phoebe to jump.

"Bishop! Don't keep blowing me off, Bishop!" A red-faced man came up behind them and Shane stepped forward, careful to keep the man from getting too close to Phoebe. She appreciated the gesture. The guy was big.

"Tim, I've told you already, the next time we talk, it's going to be in front of a judge if you keep this up."

"Screw you, Bishop! You think you're so high and mighty, walking around here like you own the damned place, like you can control other people's lives. Fuck you. Fuck you and your high and mighty freaking legal bullshit." The man poked a fat finger into Shane's chest.

Shane didn't appear to be ruffled at all. He waited a beat before speaking and when he did, his voice was low, controlled. "Tim, take your hand off me and take yourself home. Calm yourself down, then call your lawyer. If you have a problem with the restraining order, you need to take it up with your lawyer and let him explain your options to you."

Phoebe barely had time to step backward when she saw the man's fist come up. One minute the man was inches away from hitting Shane and the next minute Shane had him flat on his back with his arm in some kind of hold and a squeal coming from him. A string of curses followed the squeal as several people came out of the diner offering help.

"We're fine," Shane said as he stood. "Tim just came over to talk and he fell."

It was abundantly clear to everyone that Tim hadn't fallen down, but Phoebe realized Shane was giving him an out. A way to get out of the situation without airing his dirty laundry to everyone.

Tim glared, as Shane offered a hand to help him up. The other man stood without the help and stalked in the other direction, shaking off anyone who tried to talk to him.

Shane's hand was steady when he placed it on Phoebe's back as they walked toward the office.

"What was that about?" She whispered when they were out of earshot. She was still a little shaky from watching it. She couldn't imagine how Shane was so unaffected.

"Tim's going through a rough time. We represent his wife in their divorce. He isn't exactly in agreement about the need for a divorce and he's been harassing her." He looked back over his shoulder. "Honestly, I was surprised when he started all this. I used to think he was a good guy, but he's gotten so out-of-hand, I had to get her a restraining order a few days ago. He's a little ticked off, it seems."

They rounded the corner onto Jefferson Avenue, where the law office was located and he dropped the hand on her back. She missed its presence.

Shane shook his head. "I'll call his lawyer and see if he can get Tim settled down. I'd hate to see this escalate, but at this point, I have to watch out for Maryann."

"That's his wife?"

"Yeah."

"Any kids?" Phoebe asked. She always hated hearing about kids being caught in the battle between divorcing couples. Of course, maybe she'd have liked it better if that had been her reality growing up, instead of knowing she'd had a mother who simply hadn't cared enough to fight for her. Her own mother had never tried to visit, never tried to contact her.

"No. They were only married for a year. I guess kids haven't come into the picture yet."

They reached the law firm steps and he opened the door for her with a sigh. "Sorry about that."

Thirty minutes later, when he poked his head into her office, he pulled out the journal that had been among Fiona's belongings.

"What's up?" She eyed the journal as Shane handed it across her desk to her.

"I was thinking. Maybe you could read this. See if there's, well, I don't know. Maybe see if it gives you any ideas for a way to get through to Emmaline."

Phoebe took the journal and looked down at it, not sure what to say. She wanted to read it, for some reason, but she couldn't really say why.

"I just think it would be nice if there was some way we could help Emmaline come around to hearing her mom's words. Hearing whatever message her mom wanted her to hear. I thought it might start with reading that." He gave a nod to the journal and left.

Phoebe opened to the first page, scanning it quickly in the soft afternoon light that came in through her window.

June 28, 2006 Emmaline is still so angry with me. I'm not sure I know how to make her understand, and I don't want to do anything to make her hate her father. There isn't any reason for her to hate Aengus.

He never did abuse me or treat me poorly. It was more that he never let me be me, but I don't fault him for that, either. It was what it was. There's something about going from your father's house to your husband's house that means you never learn to stand on your own two feet. You never learn who you are and what you want. Life becomes simply about caring for other people's wants. I know that Aengus probably thinks he was only ever taking care of me, in his own way.

T'is empowering to learn to take care of yourself. Empowering to figure out who you are or who you want to be. I know now that I love painting even though I'm horribly dreadful at it. And I hate gardening. Why I thought I gave a fig for it all those years, I'll never know. Maybe because the garden was an escape. It was my place. A place no one else could control. But who has the time for all that weeding and watering and nurturing once you don't need that escape?

In a sense, every day is an escape for me now. Or maybe it's that I no longer have anything to escape from.

Aengus is angry, too, but for him it's his pride that's hurt. I don't think it ever occurred to him to think I might not be happy with him. And maybe that's my fault for never telling him. I think that most of the fault in this, if there is in fact any need to assign blame, is mine.

Going to try yoga this week. Also going to focus on forgiveness. Forgiving myself for not being perfect. Maybe if I can forgive myself, Emmaline will forgive me someday.

8

A soul that knows love knows true joy.

— FIONA O'MALLEY'S JOURNAL

June Leary was one of the Sweater Sets but also one of the Junes. There were two Junes. June Leary and June Jubie. Yes, her parents really did that to her.

It was June Leary who was currently stroking a manicured fingernail up Shane's arm. And it was doing squat for him besides remind him why he didn't want one of the Sweater Sets. He'd once thought he did. It went with his plans for stability.

Shane wasn't an idiot. He didn't need a shrink to tell him this all stemmed back to his father. Jim Bishop had been famous in this town before he'd struck gold on the two patents for industrial glue that had made the family rich. He'd been famous simply by virtue of being one of the

Bishop family, a family that could trace its roots back to when the town was initially settled in the late 1800s.

He'd been even more famous, or maybe infamous was the right term, because he was a rancher who would rather fiddle with inventions out in what his family called his "tinker barn" than tend to his cattle. For their mother, May Bishop, this had been who her husband was. It was why she loved him. For Cade and Shane, it meant watching their mother stress over how to feed the family and how to buy the new clothes the boys needed. Shane would bet Cade wasn't as affected by it as he was. For whatever reason, it had always seemed to hit Shane harder.

So he'd taken the concepts of responsibility, reliability, and doing what was expected to the extreme. For a long time, he thought that also meant marrying one of the Sweater Sets and having two point five children, or whatever the national average was for the time. He also drove a sedan. A sedate sedan, Cade always called it. And he was right. It was sedate. It was safe.

And it turned out the car and all of Shane's other life choices was leaving him restless.

"I was thinking we could get together again now that you aren't seeing Mindy. We had fun, didn't we?" June was pouting now in a way he was sure she thought was seductive. Had he ever thought it was seductive?

Probably.

He took hold of her hand, if only to stop her from the damned annoying dance of the fingernail on his bicep, which is where she seemed to be working her way to.

"I'm sorry, June. I've just been really busy." And he'd lost interest. Shane's eyes strayed to the window of the diner. Phoebe was outside talking to Shane's sister-in-law, Laura.

June followed his gaze and it would have been hard to miss the disappointment that flashed in her eyes. "And you've moved on," she said, quietly.

"I'm sorry, June." He wasn't sure why he was apologizing. It just seemed the thing to do.

She gave him a resigned smile. "I've got to run."

Shane nodded and followed her out a minute later, smiling at the two women on the sidewalk as he did. Phoebe and Laura both returned his smile and Laura came in for a hug.

"Tell me, Shane," Laura said as she pulled back and nodded down the street at a woman coming out of one of the empty buildings. "Is she leasing this time?"

Shane looked toward the woman and then shook his head at Laura. "You know I'm not going to share anything about that. Go ask her yourself."

Laura huffed. "I will. I'll get Ashley to drive out to the farm with me."

Shane grinned. "Don't let her dad hear you call it a farm." He turned to Phoebe. "That's Presley Royale. Her dad owns Royale Stables. It's killing Laura not to know why Presley is looking at commercial property in town."

Laura laughed. "I can't help it. I'm dying to know, and even Ashley doesn't seem to have the dirt this time, but I know you must. You know everything."

Shane shook his head. "*If* I know, it's because of a confidential transaction I'm not able to discuss."

Laura grinned and bumped her shoulder against

Shane's arm.

"Where's little bit, by the way?" He asked, referring to his niece, Jamie.

"With big bit. They're waiting on a litter of puppies."

"Puppies?" There was a pretty adorable thread of hope in Phoebe's voice.

Laura smiled. "Yes. One of the rescues Cade works with asked us to foster a pregnant mom. She's in labor right now."

"I don't think I'd do well with the labor part. Too much blood and all that, but I'm happy to come help with the puppies after you guys clean them all up and everything."

Shane and Laura both laughed at Phoebe and her cheeks flushed. "What? Who wants to handle the bloody part?"

"I have to agree with her on this one. Hey," Shane said, "you should come to dinner on Sunday at my mom's. You can see the puppies then."

"Oh, you should," Laura put in. "You'll love May, and I know she's been wanting to meet you."

"Good. That's settled," Shane said, somehow not wanting to give Phoebe the chance to say no. "I need to go buy a new car. Do you want to come with me?"

Phoebe blinked back at him, but Laura was the one to answer. "You're buying a new car? What's wrong with the car you have now?"

Laura looked down the street toward the law office, as though she might see his car sitting in the small lot behind the building. They all knew she couldn't see the building, let alone the car from there.

"I'm tired of it. I thought I might get something different."

"You realize I drive a canary yellow VW beetle with daisies painted on the outside?" Phoebe's look said he was an idiot. "Why on earth would you want me to help you choose a car?"

"Do you really?" There was a hint of envy in Laura's question.

"She does. It has eyelashes, too. And that's why I want your help. I need something a little more fun than a sedan."

"The Sedate Sedan," Laura put in.

Phoebe quirked a brow. "The Sedate Sedan?"

"It's what Cade calls it." Laura's dimples came out when she smiled and Shane couldn't help but laugh at his sister-in-law. If Cade had been there making fun of his sedate sedan, he'd have been tempted to hit him, but Laura could get away with anything as far as Shane was concerned. He never would have guessed he'd love having a sister as much as he did.

"I'm not saying I'm willing to go the canary yellow route, but I could probably use someone with me who can push me a little in that direction."

Phoebe shrugged. "Okay. I'm your girl."

Shane's chest tightened a little at that, but he wasn't sure what to do with it, so he ignored it.

"Great. Do you want to come, Laura?"

"Wait, we're going now? It's the middle of the workday." Phoebe looked at Laura as though she might have an answer for her, then back to Shane again. "You want to go now?"

"I do. I'll write a note for your boss if he's an ass about it."

"Funny. Very funny." Phoebe looked back to Laura. "Want to come?"

Laura raised her hands. "Sorry. Much as I'd love to see this, I'm meeting Justin for a working lunch. We've got a fundraiser to plan." Justin was Laura's brother-in-law from her first marriage. It was a marriage that had been horribly abusive. When Justin discovered what had been happening to Laura after her husband died, he'd asked her to co-found an organization to help battered women leave their spouses.

As Phoebe and Shane walked back to the law firm, she bumped him with her shoulder and looked up at him with that grin that told him she was up to no good. "I'm thinking maybe lime green or maybe Inka orange."

"Inka orange?"

"It's a color."

"I'll take your word for it."

"Trust me."

"I don't."

"You asked for my help."

"I'm beginning to think I might be suffering from periodic bouts of insanity."

She shoved at him again, but he smiled. She made him do that a lot and it felt good. Damned good.

"Mystichrome," she said, a whisper of awe playing on the words as she raised her hands in that *let me paint you a picture* way a con man might.

"I don't want to know."

9

Leap.

— Fiona O'Malley's Journal

"I'm not sure you're embracing the change," Phoebe said an hour later when Shane continued to be lured toward the gray Audi. "That's just a nicer sedan."

"But it's a really nice sedan. And it's in great shape. Once you drive a new car off the lot, you lose something like half its value. It makes sense to choose from the used cars."

"Oh my God. It's like you can't even help yourself." She stared at him, wondering how he'd come this far in life without someone to push him toward the fun every now and then. He'd brought her straight to the used car section of the dealership, and she didn't necessarily have a problem with that. It did make sense. But everything inside her was telling her he needed to let loose here and do something that didn't make sense.

He shrugged and looked at the Audi again.

"Honestly." Phoebe shook her head. "I think you should give me a budget and go wait outside while I choose."

Now it was his turn to gape. "You want me to leave and let you choose a car for me?"

She didn't even acknowledge the insanity of the suggestion. She had a hand on his shoulder pushing him out the door of the dealership. "Yeah. I think that's the way to go."

Within seconds, she had Shane standing outside the glass door, with her on the inside. She held up her phone. "Text me your budget. And any hard no's," she added in an afterthought. Not that she'd listen to them. This man needed someone to help loosen him up.

Phoebe turned and found the salesman gawking at her as well. She put her hands on her hips. "It's for his own good."

"Whatever you say, lady."

She looked down at her phone as the first of several texts came through.

You can spend up to 60k.

Her brows went up, part at the price and part at the fact he was letting her do this. She hadn't really expected him to go through with it. Of course, he could back out at any point. They were a long way from signing a contract.

And no two-seaters. Have to be able to have passengers.

She rolled her eyes. There he went thinking again.

He sent a few other texts, but she chose to ignore them as she turned to the salesman. There were only a handful of cars in the building. The rest of the used cars were in a lot out back. "Let's get out there and find the man a car."

She'd almost said *my man*, but caught herself in time, acknowledging he wasn't anything of the sort

Shane had already given the salesman the keys to his old car to look it over for a trade-in. Phoebe scanned the used car lot before turning to the newer vehicles. The dealer sold Jaguars, Volvos, and Land Rovers on the new side of the lot. She actually liked Volvos, but that wouldn't push Shane far enough out of his comfort zone.

No, he needed either a Land Rover or a Jaguar.

She pointed to a Jaguar F-Pace in a color just shy of black. It was sort of a smoky gray. "That one."

The dealer seemed to be getting in the mood for spending someone else's money. He tilted his head and eyed the car, then looked back at her with a nod. "I can see him in that."

Phoebe nodded. So could she.

One hour later, she did.

"I still can't believe you let me pick out your car." She ran her hands over the leather interior. There was nothing about the car she didn't love.

Shane eyed her from the driver's seat as he drove them back toward Evers. "I still can't believe you picked one I like so much. I'm pretty sure I wouldn't have looked at it if you hadn't picked it. Of course, since I've driven it off the lot now, I just lost half its value, but I can probably get over that."

Phoebe snorted. "Just be thankful it's not lime green."

"Oh, I am." Shane steered the car into a restaurant and Phoebe realized where they were. It was an upscale bistro that sat on riverside property thirty minutes outside of Evers.

"Fancy." Phoebe said as they got out of the car.

"I deserve to be spoiled," Shane said. "I've been working really hard and I just got a new car. What better excuse?"

"Glad to hear it's all about you."

He laughed as he took her hand in his and pulled her toward the restaurant. "Something tells me if I told you I was spoiling you, you'd run, so I'm covering."

"Sneaky."

"Whatever it takes."

10

———

You'll never plow a field by turning it over in your mind.

— IRISH PROVERB RECORDED IN FIONA O'MALLEY'S
JOURNAL

Cade was right. Shane was turning into a teenaged girl. He knew it was bad when he started fantasizing that he and Phoebe could make a relationship work. His fantasy came complete with them running the law firm together as partners rather than employer and employee.

It was just a fantasy, though. He was smart enough to know he was skirting the limits of what he should be doing with his employee. The problem was, he was just so damned tired of doing everything right. Of being the one to keep things the way they were supposed to be all the time. The one to point out where the line was and make sure they all stayed on the right damned side of it.

Because he was having a better time with Phoebe at

lunch than he'd had on any date in a long time. Scratch that. Any date ever.

Didn't that just suck since this wasn't a date? Couldn't be a date.

Knowing that didn't stop the want, though.

"Thank you for lunch," Phoebe said as they walked back out to his car. She was quieter than usual and he guessed she could feel the tension that had to be rolling off him in waves. It hadn't been there through the whole meal. It was only in the last few minutes after her hand had brushed his and he'd started to admit to himself that he was feeling a hell of a lot more here than he should be.

"You're welcome." What he didn't say hung between them.

He walked her to the passenger side of the car and opened the door for her, all the while telling himself yet again that it wasn't a date.

He was doing a piss poor job of listening.

And then Shane did the dumbest thing he'd done in a long time.

He caught Phoebe's wrist in his hand as she moved to lower herself into the seat, holding her pinned in place between him and the car.

She froze, looking up at him and he saw her breath catch. Her mouth was full and sweet and looked so damned lush he didn't want to stop himself from tasting her. Probably couldn't have even if he'd tried.

Her hand came up as he lowered his head and he stilled, waiting to see if she would stop him. If she planned to push him away. She didn't.

She pulled his head down to meet hers.

She tasted better than he'd thought she could. Better than any woman ever had and the kiss hit him like a ton of bricks. This wasn't light and easy and casual the way he thought it might be. It surged through him, stoking the need instead of slaking it.

He pulled her in closer, wrapping his arms around her as she melted into him. A low moan left his chest as he deepened the kiss and gave himself over to this woman he had no business being with.

She answered with a soft sigh that cranked his arousal up a notch higher, putting him into a dangerous zone.

Somewhere in the distance, a car door slammed and voices floated to them as other customers crossed the lot. The reminder of the world outside the kiss was enough to rip him from the fog.

Shane stepped back, hands dropping to his sides in tight fists. What the hell had he been thinking?

"I'm sorry. I shouldn't—" He didn't finish the sentence. Only stepped back, then turned and moved to the other side of the car, getting in and reaching to start the car as he called himself every name in the book.

He was turning out to be unbelievably stupid today.

11

Honey is sweet but don't lick it off a briar.

— IRISH PROVERB RECORDED IN FIONA O'MALLEY'S
JOURNAL

"Phoebe." Phoebe's best friend waved a hand in front of her face. "You still with me?"

Phoebe snapped out of the memory she'd been replaying again and again in her head. "I'm sorry! What did I miss?"

Chelsea set down her wine glass and paused the television. They were watching *A Knight's Tale* for the fifth time because Phoebe had asked for it again and Chelsea had given in, like only a best friend would. Chelsea had driven all the way from Austin for the weekend, and Phoebe couldn't shake out of the stupor Shane had put her in long enough to enjoy the visit.

She wasn't usually such a horrible friend. In fact, there'd

been a time she would have been able to put on a false front and go out dancing. Not that Evers had any spots for dancing.

"Okay, spill. What is it?" Chelsea gave her the kind of look that said she wasn't getting out of talking.

The problem was, Phoebe felt foolish. No matter how close she and Chelsea were, she couldn't help feeling foolish for lusting after her boss. The kiss the day before had made it clear he'd been lusting after her as well. Then again, he'd also stopped the kiss abruptly and told her how stupid it was to have done it.

"Hey," Chelsea ducked her head, trying to see into Phoebe's face, her voice now soft with concern. "What could be so bad, you don't want to tell *me* about it?"

"I'm falling for my boss. Hard. Really, very, extremely hard."

"Oh honey." Chelsea didn't need to explain the comment. The two friends had years' worth of history between them. Chelsea knew better than Phoebe did that she had a pattern of choosing the wrong guy.

"I know. Stupid doesn't begin to describe it. I just don't know what to do. I've tried talking myself out of it. I've tried telling myself it's natural that I'd have a little crush on him. I mean, the man's gorgeous. But that doesn't mean it's any more than a crush."

"And it doesn't mean it's not a bad idea," Chelsea said quietly. "An abysmally bad idea." She wasn't one to pull punches.

Phoebe nodded her head and swallowed. "He kissed me."

"No!"

"Yes. And then he apologized and said it was a mistake."

There was nothing but quiet in response. A good solid several minutes passed before Chelsea spoke. "Was it good?" She asked the question in a whisper.

Phoebe gave something of a half laugh, half whimper. "Yes. No. Good couldn't begin to describe it."

"Like, whole-body-goodness kind of good?"

"Yeah. And a little rock-your-world kind of goodness, too. And then he said it was a mistake."

"I'm sorry, sweetie."

"I know."

"Can I tell you something, though, without you getting mad at me?" Chelsea didn't look convinced Phoebe had it in her to make the promise, and Phoebe wasn't sure if she should be offended by that or not.

"Okay," she said slowly.

"I think you're doing this on purpose. Again."

"Doing what? I haven't dated my boss in the past. Well, I mean, I have, but only because I was dating someone and they offered me a job. But I've never started dating someone I wasn't already dating when I took the job."

"That's not what I mean." Chelsea pulled a pillow onto her lap and held it like it might offer some protection as she spoke.

Phoebe couldn't help but want her own protection.

"I think you're going for a guy you know you can't have a real lasting relationship with."

Phoebe let the words sink in. She was honest enough with herself to at least try to assess their veracity.

Chelsea continued softly. "What happened with Michael was inevitable. I think you didn't want to see it, though. Well, that's not entirely true. I think you saw it on one level but wouldn't let yourself acknowledge it."

Michael had been Phoebe's boyfriend for eighteen months before she'd gone with him to his friend's wedding. She'd been thinking about how beautiful it all was. She'd looked at little details the couple had chosen and thought maybe she and Michael would do something one way or another when they got married.

Then Michael had leaned over and whispered how lucky he was to be with a woman who wouldn't shove marriage down his throat and choke him with it the way the bride had done. "Not everyone has to get married, you know?" He'd looked at her, nodding, like he fully expected her to nod with him. She hadn't. She'd been crushed.

"I thought Michael and I were on the same page," Phoebe said, protesting Chelsea's armchair diagnosis. She really had. She'd been stunned when she realized he had truly believed she wanted nothing to do with marriage.

Chelsea narrowed her eyes. "Did you really? I mean, I know you think you did, but if you really think about it, did you really?"

Phoebe shook her head and laughed even though she didn't really feel like laughing. "That was a lot of reallys and a lot of thinks."

Chelsea raised a brow. She was never one for letting a person slip out of a conversation just because things got uncomfortable. "I think you've been running a little scared and I think it has to do with your mom. As much as you say you want marriage and a family, I think on some level, you're afraid you won't be able to cut it and you'll take off like your mom did. It's possible you've chosen guys who are either emotionally unavailable or—in the case of your boss —otherwise unattainable."

Phoebe let her head fall back.

"Too much?" Chelsea asked.

"No." Phoebe held out her wine glass. "Not enough. Wine that is. More wine. Less talk. I don't think I'm ready for psychoanalysis yet."

"Sorry," Chelsea said, refilling Phoebe's wine glass.

Phoebe looked at the glass, then back at her friend. "You know what we need?" She picked up the remote and flicked off the movie as she spoke. A sappy love story was *not* her friend at the moment.

"What's that?" Chelsea's grin said she was ready to put the psychoanalysis aside for happier things at the moment, too.

"Pie. Two Sisters Diner has the best pie you've ever tasted, and they're open late. Let's go eat pie." This time, she grinned at her friend, and Chelsea grinned back. Pie was one thing they could both always get into.

12

I'm afraid I'm going to have to be brave enough to start again.

— FIONA O'MALLEY'S JOURNAL

Phoebe curled up with Fiona O'Malley's journal Sunday afternoon after Chelsea had started the trip home. She'd already peeked between the pages earlier in the week, but hadn't had the time or energy to dig in yet. Too much of her energy had gone toward overanalyzing a kiss and an apology for the same kiss.

Now, she found herself getting lost in the heartache of a woman who had fallen in love with her husband at only sixteen years old. What should have been romantic—the high school sweetheart kind of romantic—had turned out to be something else altogether. Fiona wasn't religious about writing in her journal. She called her entries "weekly" but they were often monthly and sometimes a lot longer stretches went between.

It was almost like reading about someone trying to learn to be an adult all over again in her fifties. Fiona O'Malley had gone from living with her parents to living with her husband, who it turned out was six years older than her.

July 15, 2006 Yoga sucks.

July 23, 2006 Pilates is worse.

August 18, 2006 It turns out, it's all exercise. All exercise officially sucks.

Coffee is good, though. My mam would spin a circle in her grave if she knew I was drinking coffee instead of tea, but I've got a taste for it now. The diner has good enough coffee, and I've taken to going there after the dreaded yoga for coffee and the homemade coffee cake the sisters who own the place make. I like this little town. It's farther away from Emmaline than I'd like, but it suits me. The pace is slower and I don't have to be something I'm not here. No one seems to have expectations. I don't anyway. Besides, I'm not sure Emmaline couldn't use a little space from me right now.

December 12, 2006 New neighbor moved in next door. Beverly something-or-other. Oh, did I mention I bought the house? The divorce isn't final yet but Aengus seems to have given up fighting. Honestly, aside from the bruise to his pride, I think he might have been relieved when I left. I'm pretty sure I wasn't the only one who wasn't being themselves all these years. There is still love in my heart for him, but it's no more love than one has for a dear longtime friend. I'm thankful that I do have that for him, at least.

There were no long drawn out battles. No bitter fights. Not that we didn't have any fights over the years. We did. But in the end, there was simply a slow falling out of love. The kind that happens so gradually, you never see it happening. You only wake up one day to realize it's happened.

December 18, 2006 *Beverly is just what I need. She likes wine and coffee as much as I do and thinks yoga is for the birds. No, really, she has this flock of crazy birds that seem to be doing yoga out on the porch railing. She's thinking of making a scarecrow right there on the porch to scare them off. Birds doing yoga creep her out, and I'm sure I agree with her. We've taken to having coffee in the mornings together and wine in the afternoons. I'm still trying to find my thing. Her thing is knitting. Not for me. Maybe glass blowing. I wonder what kind of equipment one needs for glass blowing?*

January 1 2007 *Turns out, glass blowing takes a lot of equipment. Not happening.*

Emmaline chose her major. Finance. That sounds a little dry to my mind, but it's her life and I'll not live it for her.

March 13, 2007 *My divorce is final. I cried more than I thought I would. Not for me or for Aengus. Some for Emmaline, and mostly for the young couple who'd thought their love would last forever. I cried for those two, whoever they were.*

Phoebe dozed off reading and was awakened by a text alert. It took a minute to find her phone and shake off the dream she'd been having. It was a dream she'd had again and again. She dreamed her father was rocking her as a baby. He sat in a large rocking chair, one large enough to hold his strong frame. She was tiny, probably only a few weeks old, wrapped in the white and pink striped blanket the hospitals send new parents home with. He stood and set her down on the rocking chair on her back, laying a bottle by her side.

She began to squall but he walked away, only turning with a smile and a wave. He always pointed to the bottle, as if to say *you have your bottle, you'll be fine.*

The dream always left her feeling confused and alone, especially since her father had never left her. He'd been the one to stay. He had held her and rocked her and fed her. He'd been there when she was sick, when she lost her first tooth, when she figured out Santa Claus wasn't real and hated him for lying to her, when she'd had her heart broken by Billy Carver in the tenth grade, when she'd fallen off a horse and broken her ankle. Through all of it. He'd never left her.

Phoebe swiped at tears. It was utterly ridiculous. She didn't cry over her mom leaving her anymore. In fact, the times she'd cried over it had only ever really been the times she was mad at her father, or when some mother-daughter thing was going on at school. But, somehow, that dream always returned and it always left Phoebe in tears.

She lifted her phone and saw a text from Shane.

Pick you up for dinner in an hour?

Phoebe froze. She'd forgotten all about dinner at his family's house. She should make an excuse. Chelsea was right. She had no business getting personally involved in Shane and his life.

But it had been Laura and the puppies that had prompted the invite. And as far as Phoebe had heard, the Bishop Sunday dinner invitation was one that was shared frequently and widely. Almost everyone in town had had supper with the family at one time or another. It was almost an initiation into the town of sorts.

Phoebe swung her legs around and sat up. *Sure. See you then,* she texted back. She could do this. In fact, it would be a good chance to put things back on employer/employee footing for them. She'd keep the conversation to topics related to work and keep everything professional. She'd look at the puppies with Laura and make the visit about settling into town instead of settling into Shane's life. Because *that* was one thing she most definitely wasn't doing.

No. She needed to be like Fiona O'Malley had said in her journal. She needed to be focused on herself. On finding her way in the world and figuring out who she was. Then, when she'd done that, she could find a man who wasn't emotionally unavailable and who wasn't otherwise out-of-bounds, as Chelsea had said. A man who wasn't Shane Bishop.

13

Love is worth the fear. The plunge. The leap.

— Fiona O'Malley's Journal

Phoebe tried to ignore the tension that hung in the air as Shane opened the car door for her. She wasn't imagining it. It was there plain as day. The reminder of what had happened the last time they'd stood in that spot was a little too raw.

They drove in near silence.

"Is it very far from town?" She asked when it was clear this wasn't going to be one of those comfortable silences two people could enjoy without needing to fill.

"Not far. Twenty minutes. I think Ashley and Garret will be there, and probably her sister Cora."

"I haven't met Cora yet, but I like Ashley a lot."

Shane laughed. "It's hard not to like Ashley. She tells you

exactly what she's thinking all the time. It could be obnoxious, I guess, but she somehow makes it work for her."

The heaviness in the air lightened as they chatted and he told her about Ashley's friend and one of the town's most cherished fixtures: Hadeline Gertrude Gillman.

"Ms. Haddie and Ashley are almost a matching set, with the exception of the difference of some fifty years or so between them. Sometimes I think they're competing to see who can shock people the most. Neither has an internal filter. If we're lucky, Ms. Haddie will be at dinner. Believe me, the entertainment value of the two of them together can't be beat."

He was right. It was apparent the minute they arrived and people poured out onto the porch to great them. Above a cacophony of chatter as introductions were made and hugs exchanged, the white-haired woman Phoebe had just been introduced to as Ms. Haddie, took one look at Shane's new car and called out. "Your sedan looks a little swollen. Did someone beat it about the head with a baseball bat?"

Ashley shook her head at Ms. Haddie. "It's just a sprain. It'll be back to usual after ice, elevation, and rest."

Shane grinned. "Funny, you two. Phoebe picked it out."

All heads swiveled her way and Phoebe felt the urge to hide. It had been funny when she'd talked him into letting her choose the car, but now it seemed intimate. Too intimate.

"I, um..." She looked to Shane for help, then back at the car.

There was silence as she flailed for something to say. Ashley moved in before she could come up with anything, looping her arm through Phoebe's and tugging her toward the barn while she tipped her head toward Laura. "Let's go show Phoebe the adorable puppies."

"You hate the puppies," Laura said.

"Hate is a very strong word, but more importantly, I want to talk to her alone." Ashley said this with no effort to keep the rest of the group from hearing her. Oddly, Phoebe understood what Shane had meant. It was hard not to grin as Ashley manhandled her down to the barn where the puppies were, even as her cheeks heated knowing Shane was probably being grilled.

Laura and Ashley chatted on the way to the barn, as though they weren't about to give her the third degree.

"Did you talk to Presley?" Laura asked.

"Yes!" Ashley said this in a voice that said the story she had was a juicy one. "She's leasing the building across from Katelyn's studio. She's going to open a coffee shop!"

"What?" Laura didn't ask this as a question. It was more surprise than anything.

"She's the horse girl?" Phoebe asked. She was more than happy to let Presley Royale's coffee shop derail their train of thought if it meant getting her out of the hot seat.

"Yep," Laura said, then turned to Ashley as she pushed open the barn doors. "What does her dad have to say about that?"

Ashley shook her head. "We're sworn to secrecy. She said I could tell you and Katelyn, and I'm assuming she'd be okay with Phoebe, but you guys can't tell anyone yet." She looked over at Phoebe and Phoebe made a cross-your-heart gesture over her chest.

Ashley nodded and continued. "Her dad doesn't know yet. Presley is retiring."

"She'd not going to ride anymore?" Laura asked, but Phoebe had tuned the other women out.

She just about turned to mush at the sight of ten wiggling, wriggling blobs of fur lying in the barn stall Laura had led them to. The puppies were all black like their mother, who looked up with deep black eyes and a tail that thwacked the ground as she wagged it. She lay on her side, most of the puppies clamoring for a spot to nurse.

The sound that came involuntarily from Phoebe was part squeal, part sigh, and all happiness. "They're so beautiful."

"They smell funny." Ashley wrinkled her nose as Laura hit her with a light backhanded slap to the shoulder.

"Where did they come from?" Phoebe asked as she sank down and watched the puppies try to crawl on legs that weren't ready for it yet. "It's like heaven." She scooped a puppy up, its eyes still closed, and brought it to her nose. Puppy breath was like crack, she decided. And she needed more hits. Lots of them.

Phoebe heard laughter and looked up at Laura and Ashley, who was flat out snorting at her.

Ashley stopped laughing to explain. "Well, sweetheart, when two dogs really love each other, they share a special kind of hug."

Laura elbowed Ashley, but she was smiling, too. "You're so damned obnoxious."

"She walked right into that one."

"I really did," Phoebe said as Laura sat next to her.

Ashley chose to sit on a nearby tack box, presumably to avoid the puppy attack that was inevitable on the ground. "What I meant," she said with a laughing glance toward Ashley, "is where did you get the mom? Is she a rescue?"

"Yes. Cade works with all kinds of rescued animals. Most of the time, we get animals who've been mistreated. He has a way of reaching them when others can't."

"He whispered Laura right on into his heart when she came to the farm." Now Ashley sighed wistfully and Phoebe didn't think she was joking about how romantic she thought it was. "It was so sweet."

"It was." Laura's smile was wide and it reached her eyes. In fact, it reached her whole being. She seemed to glow as she talked about her husband. Phoebe felt a pang of longing for that kind of relationship. "Well, once I got past the fact that I knew he was applying all of his dog training tricks on me. If you can look past that, it was very romantic."

A tiny set of teeth clamped down on Phoebe's thumb and she yelped before removing the culprit from her lap. "Sharp little buggers."

"All right, we've let you put this off long enough. First, we need your story. Why you're here, what your hang ups are, and all that. Then, give us the dirt on you and Shane." Ashley looked up at Laura. "Or do we want the Shane story first then the backstory? What do you think?"

Laura's only response was to shake her head at her friend, a look of tolerant love in her eyes.

Phoebe couldn't help but laugh. "It's a boring story, really. I moved here from Austin when I realized my life—

and my relationship with a guy I'd been dating for over a year—was headed nowhere."

"Couldn't commit, huh? Men are like that." Ashley nodded sagely.

"This from the woman happily married to a wonderfully committed hottie," Laura put in.

"You and I, my friend, have found *the* guys. They're like a subspecies. Hard to locate, but once you cull them from the herd, they're yours to keep." Ashley paused. "I have to say, I really think Shane is one of *the* men. He's all about commitment, if that's what you're looking for."

Phoebe chose to study the squirmy mass of love in her lap instead of meeting the women's eyes. "Except, to me, he's also one of those unavailable men. My friend, Chelsea, thinks I'm choosing men like that on purpose. Men I can't have for whatever reason. In the case of my ex, he was emotionally unavailable. Happy to have me in his life, so long as I didn't ask for too much or expect it to go anywhere past that. With Shane, he's unattainable because I work for him."

"Just because you work with Shane doesn't have to mean he's unavailable. You're both adults. If it doesn't work out, you agree to be professional about it and you work together, the same as you always have," Ashley said.

Phoebe and Laura both gave her looks that said they weren't buying her maturity act.

"You think you could have done that with Garret if things hadn't worked out?" Laura challenged. "I think I would have had a hard time if I had to work with Cade if things didn't work out with us."

"He kissed me. Then apologized. Trust me. It's awkward."

"And he let you pick out his new car." Ashley said, a sly smile taking over the dark-haired woman's features.

"It really wasn't a big deal," Phoebe said.

"Ha!" The fact this came from Laura instead of Ashley was a little surprising.

Ashley pointed to Laura. "What she said. It's a *very* big deal."

"Shane spends months researching cars when it's time for a new one. He makes charts, compares features, reviews safety reports. He doesn't turn it over to someone else."

Phoebe looked at Laura and felt her jaw drop. "He makes charts?"

Ashley shrugged and answered for Laura. "He's a little uptight."

Her mind flashed back to the kiss in the parking lot and Phoebe wanted to argue. That man was anything but uptight. He'd been hot with just that little bit of control that makes the kiss sexy as sin and lets you know he'd be the one in control in the bedroom, but in a good way. In a delicious way. Phoebe shivered and Ashley caught it, pointing a finger at her this time, waving it but not saying anything. She didn't need to say anything. Her look was saying it all.

Phoebe tipped her head back and let out a groan. "I don't know what to do. I love Evers, I love my job. It's not like there are a ton of law firms here. I can't just go find a new job if things don't work out."

"All true." Ashley nodded. "All valid, true points."

Laura looked at Phoebe. "But, if you don't see where

anything goes with him, will you still be able to keep working there, or have things already gone beyond that point?"

"Oh, yeah, okay," Ashley said with a very unhelpful nod, "that's a good point, too. She's got you there."

"You're two of the least helpful people I could have come to, aren't you?"

Laura and Ashley laughed at that, but Laura was quick to offer a sad smile. "I'm sorry. I don't think there's an easy answer here."

Phoebe looked down at the now-sleeping pile of fur in her lap. Maybe she could just stay here with the puppies and not face the real world.

Yeah. Puppies good. World bad.

14

May the roof above you never fall in and those gathered beneath it never fall out.

— IRISH PROVERB RECORDED IN FIONA O'MALLEY'S JOURNAL

P hoebe went back to the journal as soon as she climbed into bed that night. So far, nothing in it indicated Fiona was a woman who would consider committing suicide. Even when she and her daughter were not getting along, Fiona seemed determined to push through life, finding the good instead of looking for the bad.

Of course, she wasn't routine in her writing. Maybe the periods where the journal entries stopped were times she was depressed or dealing with things she couldn't face head on.

But Phoebe didn't think so. Fiona inspired her with her

strength and her ability to see good in herself and those around her.

January 1, 2010 Bet you thought I was gone for good. I've been a little remiss in my writing. I've been busy. It turns out, finding a hobby wasn't the key to finding myself. Simply living with myself for a while was the key. I've learned a lot about myself.

For one thing, I like me. A lot. I'm a good friend. If I ever forget that, Beverly lets me know. She and I have started going to the senior center in town. A few of the people that go there are bat-crap crazy, but the woman who runs it is nice. Miriam Green. Honestly, she's no spring chicken herself, but she's the kind of person who likes getting everyone together for organized games. She's got that cheerleader personality. Beverly and I lack that, but we make up for our lack of cheerleading with snide comments everyone really knows are meant to be supportive.

The center gives us someplace to go. I'm beginning to realize spending my life as a homemaker left me without much to do once the people who made up the home are gone. Emmaline has begun accepting my invitations to lunch from time-to-time, but there's a void between us now that I can't seem to fill. I'd give anything to have our old relationship back. To know she loved me the way she used to love me. To know she didn't still blame me for breaking up what she always saw as a perfect family.

She likes her new job but she's thinking about going back to school for an advanced degree. She says she needs that to compete with the men in her field. I don't think she'll ever know how proud I am of her. She sees what she wants and she's going for it. No hesitation, no leaning on someone else. No holding back. I envy her that.

I'll have to figure out a way to show her how proud I am of her. I've always thought showing is more important than telling, although the telling is important, too.

Bev and I are going to make chocolate martinis on the porch soon, so I've got to run! Ta ta, dear diary!

15

It's a hard thing, to let yourself believe you are enough.

— Fiona O'Malley's Journal

"Shane?"

Shane looked up to find Margaret fanning herself in his office doorway. He scanned her from head to toe. She didn't look sick or injured, other than the fanning. "Everything okay?"

"There's someone here looking for Phoebe. I wasn't sure if I should tell him she's down at Tiny's for lunch."

"Why are you fanning yourself?" As soon as the words were out of his mouth, he wondered if he should have asked them. Maybe he didn't want to know the answer. Or maybe this was one of those situations where he was supposed to pretend he didn't see her doing it.

"You'll see." Was all she said as she turned and walked out to the lobby, apparently expecting him to follow.

He did.

A large tattooed man clad in leather from head to toe stood looking expectantly at Margaret as she walked back behind her desk. It wasn't hard to see the flush that crept up her face as the man smiled at her, and Shane would have to be an idiot not to see why. Not that he spent a lot of time looking at other men, but this guy had that look women went crazy over.

Dark hair and a scar over one eyebrow that he would bet had made him even more appealing to women rather than detracting from the man's looks. To top it off, he was large and looked like his muscles hadn't been earned in a gym. They likely came from hours of hard riding on the bike Shane would bet the man had out front.

He also had a feeling he knew exactly who he was.

"Hi, I'm Shane Bishop. Margaret tells me you're here for Phoebe." Shane cringed internally, thinking he sounded like an overprotective father. Or a dick.

The man didn't seem to notice. He grinned and offered a handshake. "Ray Eisnett. Pleasure to meet you. I was hoping to catch Phoebe, but I'm beginning to gather she's not around."

"She should be back—"

"Ray!" This was accompanied by a gasp. "What in the world?"

Shane tilted to look around the large man and saw Phoebe standing stock still in the entrance to the law firm.

"Hey, beautiful! How's my girl?" And then Ray was spinning Phoebe around in his arms with one hand on her ass, as she slapped at his shoulder to put her down.

Only she was grinning as hard as Ray was.

"You can't just pop in at my office," she hissed as the large man set her down.

"It's not a problem, Phoebe," Shane said, but he found he had to actively loosen the tension in his jaw as he smiled. "Nice to meet you, Ray."

He didn't wait to find out what the visit was about. He turned and walked back into his office, not wanting to watch the other man's hands on Phoebe a minute longer.

"Idiot." He said this to himself, but started when Margaret hissed a reply from behind him.

"He's not an idiot. He's a nice man."

"I wasn't..." He shook his head. He couldn't explain to his receptionist that he was calling himself an idiot for thinking he had any right to throw the man through the nearest wall just for touching Phoebe. "What are you doing?"

"I'm giving them some privacy," she whispered as she looked through the crack she'd left when she'd almost closed his door.

"Actually, it looks like you're not." He said this as he went and planted his ass in his desk chair. No way in hell he was going to look through that slit in the door with Margaret.

Margaret looked back at him, her brows nearly on the ceiling. "He's asking her to come back to him!"

Shane ground his teeth, remembering the conversation he'd had when he called Ray's Tattoo Parlor for a reference. The man had asked him to tell Phoebe he wanted her back. Apparently, he'd come to town to ask himself this time.

"He's kissing her!" Margaret hissed, this time, not

turning around. Apparently, she didn't want to miss the show. "Oh my God."

"What?" He asked, despite every neuron in his brain screaming at him to keep his mouth shut.

"The man can kiss, that's all. I think *I* felt that."

Shane swore under his breath.

"She pushed him away!"

It was all kinds of wrong that Shane wanted to jump up and watch this part.

Screw it. He did.

With his height and Margaret's lack of it, it was an easy matter for him to look through the door in the space above Margaret. There was Ray, holding Phoebe's hands as she shook her head at him. She put her hand on his chest and rubbed it, but there was a big brother or best friend quality to the touch.

"Good for her," Margaret whispered. "She can do better."

"A minute ago, you couldn't pick your tongue up off the floor." Shane didn't take his eyes off Phoebe and Ray. They were hugging now, and he was walking out. "Now you think she can do better?"

Margaret shut the door. "I know, but Phoebe's special. She can do much better than him."

If Margaret thought Tattoo Ray wasn't good enough for Phoebe, just who did she think would be enough?

"You can come out now, you two!" Phoebe's tone said she wasn't upset they'd been listening.

Margaret led the way. "What did he want?" She asked

the question with the air of someone who had no idea what had taken place.

Phoebe snorted. "Please, like you didn't see the entire thing."

"It was all her." Shane pointed to Margaret.

"Traitor," Margaret shot back at him.

Phoebe waved her hand at the two of them in dismissal. "Don't sweat it. Ray shows up from time to time to ask me to come back to him. The last time we actually dated was six years ago."

Shane could see that. Phoebe left an impression on a man.

Margaret grinned and pulled Phoebe closer. "Come on, admit it. Sometimes you're tempted to just climb on that Harley and take him for a ride, aren't you?"

Phoebe's cheeks colored as she burst out laughing. She was shaking her head when she walked away.

Margaret turned to Shane with a shrug. "What? I'm old. I have to live vicariously."

16

Don't put off finding yourself. The sooner you do it, the sooner you'll be able to share yourself with others.

— FIONA O'MALLEY'S JOURNAL

"You're a saint for coming." Ashley looped her arm in Phoebe's as they walked into the high school together. "Laura is busy with the puppies and Katelyn and John are having a date night."

Phoebe wasn't entirely sure she wanted to be here. "You're kind of scaring me."

Ashley laughed at that. "No, it's not so bad. Honestly, the Junes and Mindy are sweet. They don't bite at all. They just always seem so put together, you know? Sometimes, I swear they must have a makeup and wardrobe crew at their houses. I needed a real person with me for a buffer."

"Gee, thanks," Phoebe deadpanned as Ashley led her

down a long hall. The school was closed but they'd been allowed the use of the teacher's lounge for the meeting.

"Why don't you guys just use one of the rooms at the library?" Phoebe had been inside the library and it had rooms that were specifically intended for meetings. Ashley had told her they held book clubs and knitting groups, and all kinds of stuff in the library.

"Oh, June teaches at the school, and she was involved with this before I was. Since she already had this all set up, we continued it here."

Phoebe opened her mouth to ask which June, since she'd been told there were two of them, but didn't get the words out.

"Ash, you're here!"

Both women turned to see a blonde in a perfectly-coordinated skirt and top with a cardigan sweater buttoned over her shoulders. Phoebe really didn't know people did that anymore, but on this woman, it looked right.

Phoebe reached up to touch her hair where she was sure she'd find tendrils and curls slipping loose of the clips she'd put in it earlier. This woman's hair was perfect, laying just so on her shoulders, without a fly-away to be seen anywhere.

"Well, of course I am. Why wouldn't I be?" Ashley laughed. "June Leary, this is Phoebe Joy. She—"

June smiled brightly and put out her hand. "I know exactly who she is! I've been dying to meet you. We need more young people in this town. I'm June. June Leary. You'll meet my bestie, June Jubie and my other bestie, Mindy Mason, in a few minutes. I told Mindy we need to recruit you for the pageant. You'll be the perfect person to help us get the pageant off the ground."

Phoebe was surprised the woman stopped to take a breath, but she didn't have time to process anything long enough to form a response. Because Ashley was now behind June shaking her head and mouthing the word *no* in an enormously exaggerated manner.

"Oh, uh, I..."

"Don't worry." June pulled Phoebe into what looked like the teacher's lounge, with a large table in the center. "I'll tell you all about that later. Tonight, we're here to work on the summer baskets."

"We should talk about the Fall festival, too. I've got a few ideas for bringing in out-of-town authors if Ashley is willing to help us with that." Phoebe turned toward the source of the voice to see two other women who looked remarkably like June as far as style, if not looks.

The one with the hair that could more closely be called honey brown than blonde stuck her hand Phoebe's way. "I'm Mindy Mason. You must be Phoebe."

"Yes, hi, it's nice to meet you."

"I'm the other June," said the woman with the lighter hair. "June Jubie. Yes, my parents really did that to me!" She didn't seem to mind in the least as she smiled and squeezed Phoebe's hand.

The next hour and twenty minutes were spent with talk of organizing summer baskets of food and toys for local families in need. They discussed which businesses had donated what the year before, and how to get them to

100 | LORI RYAN

donate again. They talked about organizing lists of families with children who would need toys in their baskets and those without children who'd rather forego the toys for extra food. There were also ideas and plans for the Fall Festival and Phoebe truly hoped they weren't the only ones who would be running the event. It sounded like there was enough for ten people to do, not the four who sat here. Then she remembered Katelyn and Laura would normally be here, as well. Even so, the task list seemed enormous.

Ashley had been right. The Junes and Mindy were nice. They were just intense. That was the best way Phoebe could think to describe it. *Intense*. She had a feeling she saw them the same way Ashley did—as women she would be happy to be friendly with, but not women she saw herself as being *besties* with, as June had put it.

All in all, though, the evening wasn't bad and she went home feeling happy she'd come to Evers, Texas. She had had friends in Austin, of course. They'd gone to movies or concerts and restaurants together. But there wasn't this sense of community. There wasn't the sense that you could put your energy into your town and make it better in some way. That you had something worthwhile to add to it.

It felt really...well, really nice. The word wasn't nearly strong enough, but when you boiled it right down, that's what it was. Of course, since she'd just volunteered to be in charge of decorating one hundred cardboard boxes to look like baskets, she might change her mind on that. As it turned out, real baskets were too pricey to use. If they used cardboard boxes, they could shift more money to food and household goods.

"Pinterest, here I come," Phoebe murmured as she sat in front of her computer. "I am sooo going to regret this," she said to the empty room, because apparently, wrapping hundreds of yards of jute string around empty boxes was somewhere in her future.

17

There's nothing so bad that it couldn't be worse.

— IRISH PROVERB RECORDED IN FIONA O'MALLEY'S
JOURNAL

Shane looked up as Beverly Newman entered his office. He stood and crossed the room, leading her to a chair. "Hi, Beverly. Margaret said you needed to see me today, but she didn't say why."

She patted his arm as he sat in the chair next to her. "I didn't say why. What I have to talk to you about is, well, I don't want to spread it around."

Shane nodded, not arguing with Beverly. Margaret was completely trustworthy with anything that was said in the office. Their clients' confidential information was never spread around town. But there wasn't any reason to argue the point right now.

"Okay. What can I do for you?"

"I don't think Fiona killed herself. I want you to help me convince Garret to investigate her death."

Shane sat back, stunned. "Tell me why you think that."

"Well, for one thing, it just wasn't in her nature. You know that."

"I do," he said carefully. "I also know she was seeing signs of dementia and after witnessing her brother go through that, she never wanted to burden Elliot with what her brother's family went through."

Beverly nodded. "I know that. But I also know she was making plans right up until the day before she died. She was planning a surprise weekend away with Elliot for his birthday. It makes no sense to do that one day, then kill yourself the next."

Shane waited, almost certain she had more to say. He'd known Beverly for a long time, and she wasn't the type of person to tell herself something like this just because she was missing her friend, although he was sure she was.

"She and I had both talked about the dementia she was having and we agreed, it wasn't following the normal pattern of dementia."

This got his attention. "How so?"

"Dementia has stages. It begins with mild symptoms and progresses gradually from there. Fiona was experiencing a very sudden onset of moderate to severe symptoms. We agreed she should go see Dr. Allen and see if there was some reason for the sudden symptoms."

Hall Allen had taken over his father's practice the year before. He was a good doctor. He'd grown up in Evers and left for medical school and to practice in a larger city for several years before coming home to work with his father. When the senior Dr. Allen had suffered a stroke the year before, Hall had been left as the sole practitioner while his father recuperated.

"Is it possible she visited him and received a diagnosis she couldn't accept? Maybe she was sicker than you guys thought?" He wondered if something like a brain tumor could have been responsible for her symptoms. Maybe Fiona had discovered the cause and had decided she didn't want to live with it.

Beverly was shaking her head again. "No. She had an appointment with Dr. Allen this week."

Unease crept over Shane and he wondered if he'd contributed to Garret calling Fiona's death a suicide without really having all the facts.

"I know Garret is having the medical examiner do an autopsy," he said. "I can talk to him if you'd like. Make sure he knows your concerns."

Beverly clenched his hands between hers and he saw tears spring to her eyes. "This wasn't her, Shane. It wasn't her."

Shane nodded. "I'll talk to Garret." He knew Garret would never take his duty lightly. Shane wasn't ready to accept what Beverly was saying wholesale, but he could at least make sure Garret knew that not everyone assumed Fiona's death was a suicide.

18

You won't learn to swim on the kitchen floor.

— FIONA O'MALLEY'S JOURNAL

Phoebe smiled as Ashley entered her office and flopped into the chair across from her desk.

"I think your friend is wrong."

Phoebe looked blankly at Ashley, then leaned forward and looked out at the reception area. It wasn't that Phoebe minded Ashley coming in unannounced. It was just that Margaret was oddly tenacious about announcing visitors before they came into either of Shane or Phoebe's offices. In fact, it had always made Phoebe laugh. The woman seemed to think of herself as a guard dog of sorts.

Margaret looked back at her, brows raised. Phoebe leaned back in her chair, her gaze returning to Ashley.

Ashley raised a shoulder with a laugh. "She likes me."

"By all means, don't let me interrupt your train of thought. You were saying something about my friends?"

"The one who said you shouldn't bone Shane."

"Jeez, Ashley." Phoebe stood and shut her office door. "Really?"

Ashley only grinned. The woman had no shame.

Before she could shut the door all the way Laura and Katelyn scooted in.

"Wait for us," Laura said.

Shane stepped out of his office, but Laura turned and shooed him back in with her hands. "Phoebe's taking her lunch break."

"It's ten a.m., Laura," Phoebe said, but Shane just laughed and walked back into his office.

"I called them." Ashley didn't look the least bit apologetic as the girls all settled into Phoebe's office with the door shut. The room wasn't exactly large. It was about half the size of Shane's office. With three of them in chairs and Katelyn perched on the edge of the desk, it was crowded.

Yet, it felt good, Phoebe realized. She really liked this town, she thought as she scowled at Ashley.

"Oh, stop." Ashley waved her scowl away. "We need to talk and it's better if we're all here for this. I think you should sleep with Shane."

Phoebe raised her brows. "Be blunt about it, why don't you."

"Maybe you could just start with a date. Or a kiss," Katelyn said.

"They've kissed already. It was magical." Ashley didn't

seem the least bit concerned about sharing Phoebe's personal business.

"And then he apologized and said it shouldn't have happened." Phoebe felt the need to keep that in the forefront of her mind. It was one of the ways she was protecting herself against what would undoubtedly be messy and heartbreaking in the end.

"Okay, let's back up here. Why are you so convinced it would end badly?" Ashley looked to Laura and Katelyn with her question, and both women nodded their agreement.

"Statistics." Phoebe wasn't at all the kind of person to go by statistics. She was a gut instinct kind of girl if there ever was one. But, in this case, she felt she needed something concrete to hand Ashley.

"Do tell." The dryness in Ashley's tone couldn't be missed and Phoebe laughed.

"Well, look at it. How many relationships did you guys have before you found your husbands?"

"True," Katelyn put in. "I did have to go through quite a few frogs."

"I think it's toads," said Ashley wrinkling her brow.

Laura raised her hand and wiggled her fingers. "I only went through two men."

All eyes swiveled toward her, and no one needed to remind her how that first relationship had gone.

Laura shrugged her shoulders. "Just saying."

"Since none of us are buying the statistics crap," Ashley said with a glare toward Katelyn, "tell us what's really going on."

Phoebe probably shouldn't have felt comfortable

opening up to these women. In all honesty, she didn't know them well. But somehow, they had a way of setting her at ease and making her feel like they wouldn't judge or spread her story all around town. They might gossip between themselves plenty, but she didn't get the sense that they would run out and share personal details with other people.

"I think I'm just afraid." The truth of the statement struck her. She *was* afraid. And it wasn't just that she was afraid things wouldn't work out with Shane. It was that she thought they might. That he might just be the one for her, but that she might not be able to hack it, like her mother. That she wouldn't have what it took to be a wife and mother.

"I get that," Ashley said, surprising Phoebe. Ashley didn't seem like anything could frighten her. "I was deathly afraid to let Garret in. I'm glad I did though. Even if it hadn't worked out the way it did, just letting him in and giving up all the fears and doubts about being able to have a relationship with someone was life-changing for me."

Phoebe watched as Laura and Katelyn flanked Ashley, smothering her with hugs.

She wondered what Fiona O'Malley would tell her to do. She had a feeling the woman would have said to grab everything in life that she could with open arms and an open heart. She'd just started reading the sections of Fiona's journal covering the time when she met and fell in love with Elliot. She had expected Fiona to struggle with the idea of loving a man so much younger than her. Fiona had, for a very short time. It was the time in which she let her fears control her. The difference was, Fiona had looked that fear in the eye and recognized it for what it was. She had realized her fears had more to do with worry about what other people might think. When she had looked instead at how Elliot made her feel, the decision to be with him had become easy.

Living in fear is no life at all, Fiona had said.

The only problem for Phoebe, was that she didn't trust what she was feeling. No, that wasn't quite right. She didn't trust herself. She didn't trust she had what it took to let herself have what she wanted most of all. A family, happiness. Permanence.

19

It isn't the riches, the things, the property you gather around you that can make or break your day. It's the people. The friends and the loves. Value them and hold them dear.

— FIONA O'MALLEY'S JOURNAL

Shane cursed under his breath as he stared at the screen. He was out of ideas. He wanted nothing more than to be able to tell Laura where her brother was buried. When he'd made the offer a year ago, he hadn't ever imagined it would be so difficult.

His sister-in-law had been raised in a small New Jersey town by an emotionally abusive father. She and her brother, James, were tight growing up. When Laura had married her first husband, Patrick Kensington, she'd left her father and brother to lead a life that should have been the envy of every woman. The Kensingtons had money and power beyond compare. They were politically connected and influential. It was as close to marrying into royalty as one could get in the United States.

It hadn't taken long for Laura's world to be plunged from fairy tales to nightmares. In fact, it happened on her wedding night, the first of many times her husband would beat her. Laura was in the midst of the three-year hell her husband put her through when she got word her brother had died. She never had the chance to attend his funeral.

"It shouldn't be this hard." Shane had known for a while now that something wasn't adding up as far as James Lawless was concerned. No record of death seemed to exist and none of the cemeteries in the area where he and Laura were raised had a record of him being buried. No funeral home had cremated him. It was as if the man hadn't died.

"What shouldn't be so hard?"

Shane jumped at the sound of Phoebe's voice and turned to find her in the door of his office.

"Sorry," she said but the smile splitting her face said she was anything but. He loved seeing her smile, even when it was at his expense.

Her eyes danced and lit from within when she was happy. The more he saw that, the more he wanted to make her happy.

That didn't mean he at all believed her claim she was sorry for startling him. "No, you're not."

She shrugged and came to stand over his shoulder, looking at the computer screen. He was struck again by the idea of them working as partners. It wasn't the idea of having her as a partner in the firm that was really the fantasy. The fantasy was having her as a partner in life. It was powerful when it hit him, and he knew he'd give in eventually. He wasn't doing a very good job of shaking the feeling that he wanted more with Phoebe Joy.

"I'm trying to track down Laura's brother."

Phoebe frowned at the screen. "What do you mean?"

Laura was extremely open about her history, even sharing her story in talks she gave for women around the country, so Shane didn't hesitate to share it with Phoebe.

"You know she used to be Laura Kensington. That her husband abused her?"

"Yes. And he's dead now." There was a hint of satisfaction in Phoebe's voice. Shane couldn't say he blamed her.

"Right," Shane confirmed. "About six months into their marriage, her brother died. She wasn't able to attend his funeral. She and her father are estranged. The man is, well, he's horrible. He was emotionally abusive to her all her life. Her brother was her protector. I know it bothers her that she's never been able to find his grave and go say goodbye."

"That should be easy." Phoebe looked to his computer as though the answer should have appeared there by now.

He understood her response. The answer should have been easy.

Shane laughed. "Uh huh," he said, with a sideways look in her direction.

She smirked and ran through all the ways he'd already covered for locating the burial site of James Lawless.

"All done. And before you ask, yes, I googled him."

"Can you pull up the property records around their childhood home?"

Shane frowned at her but did as she asked and turned the screen so she could look at the records.

"Okay," she said pointing. "Now look up this woman and see if her phone number is available."

It took three tries but they found someone with a listed number that lived across the street from the Lawless family.

Phoebe picked up the phone and started making calls. It took several more tries before she found someone who was home and willing to talk with her.

She had the phone on speaker so he could hear. "You say you're with a law firm?" The woman sounded elderly.

"Yes. We represent a woman who grew up near you and we're trying to help her find some information on her brother. You would have known them as Laura and James Lawless if you lived in the neighborhood when they were there."

The response was immediate. "Oh, those poor kids. Horrible man, their father. We all knew he wasn't treating them right. The problem was, there wasn't anything anyone could do. Back then, there wasn't any such thing as help for kids if they weren't being physically injured. Times were different. There had to be bruises and broken bones and things."

The woman made a sound of disapproval. "And then what happened to Laura."

Phoebe murmured a response. Laura's story had been national news. She'd been in the spotlight first as one of the Kensingtons, then as the Kensington who'd been beaten.

"He's still there, you know. Holed up inside his house.

Jacob Lawless deserves to be alone in the world, and he's gotten all he deserves. He's reaped everything he's sown."

Phoebe's eyes met Shane's for a minute before she looked back at the phone. "Mrs. Parker, can you tell us what you know about James? We're trying to help Laura find his grave." Phoebe paused. "Her late husband never gave her that information, and as you can imagine, she isn't in touch with her father."

Shane had tried talking to Laura's father. He refused to answer any calls and hadn't responded to registered letters, either. He was about ready to fly out there and beat the information out of the man.

Now there was silence on the other end of the line.

"Mrs. Parker?"

"I'm here. I'm sorry. You just caught me off guard. James isn't dead. Not as far as I know. He went into the military. That was years ago and he doesn't visit, but I haven't heard anything about him since the day he left."

Shane's head shot up and he met Phoebe's eyes to find they were just as filled with surprise as his own.

"Do you know what branch of the military?" Phoebe asked.

"Well, I've always thought the Army, but I can't remember if that was told to me at one point, or if I just assumed. I'm really not sure."

"That's all right, Mrs. Parker. We can find out."

"He was a good boy, that James. A very good boy and an honorable man."

Phoebe's response was soft. "I'm sure he was. Thank you

so much. You've been a big help." Phoebe disconnected the line and held up a finger to Shane when he began to speak.

As he watched, she dialed another long-distance call from memory.

"General Brophy's office." The male voice on the other end of the line held the kind of no-nonsense tone that said you'd better have a reason for interrupting his day. Shane wondered how in the hell Phoebe happened to have a General's phone number on speed dial in her head.

"Hi Carson. Is my dad available?"

Dad was a General. That's, apparently, how you get a number like that.

It was almost comical how quickly the voice on the other end of the line softened. "Hey, Pheebs. Hang on. It's going to take me a few minutes to pull him up here."

"Thank you!" Phoebe covered the speaker of the phone with her hand and turned to Shane, obviously reading the question on his face.

"It's easier than calling his cell. Most of the time, he can't take a phone into the meetings he's in and Carson always knows exactly where he is in the building."

"What building is that?" Shane had a feeling he knew the answer, but the question just had to be asked.

She held her hands up in as close to the shape of a pentagon as one could get with their hands as the phone line came back to life.

"Pumpkin?"

Phoebe rolled her eyes. "My boss is on the line, dad. You're on speaker."

"It's a pleasure to meet you, Sir," Shane said leaning

forward. He threw a glare at Phoebe that hopefully told her not to spring a call with a General on him again. She laughed.

"And you, Shane. Phoebe's told me about you."

Shane felt like a teenager going up against his date's dad. He couldn't imagine what Phoebe's dates had gone through when they came to pick her up.

"I hope all of it was good."

The General laughed and Shane felt marginally better.

"Most of it, anyway," said General Brophy. "Are you calling to tell me my daughter is the best paralegal you've ever hired?"

Now Shane laughed. "I won't lie. She is *absolutely* the best paralegal I've ever hired."

He liked the way Phoebe flushed.

She wasn't having any more of it. "Okay, you two can carry on your little lovefest later. I'm calling for a reason, dad."

"She used to use the same tone with me when she was young. I think she gets a kick out of being the only person on the planet who can boss me around."

"True. There are a few people who outrank you, dad."

Shane's brows went up, but he heard laughter on the other end of the line.

"Okay, Pumpkin. What can I do for you?"

"We're actually calling for a friend. We've been helping her track down her brother's grave. She's estranged from their father, but she was told years ago her brother had died. We haven't been able to locate any information on him, but a neighbor just told us the brother enlisted in the Army. I was hoping you can tell us how to go about getting information for her?" Phoebe paused. "Or maybe you might look him up off the record for us?" She said this last in her best pretty-please voice.

There was a pause, but it wasn't a long one. "What's this brother's name?"

"James Lawless. The sister is Laura Bishop now. She was Laura Kensington before that."

"Hang tight."

"Really?" Shane growled to Phoebe as they waited. "You didn't want to warn me?"

She outright giggled and he shot her a look. "I sign your paychecks, you know?"

"Oh, I know." She narrowed her eyes at him.

"Phoebe?" The General sounded off when he came back on the line. His voice held a heaviness that Shane knew couldn't be good. "Your friend isn't on the call, is she?"

Shane's eyes met Phoebe's as she told her father no.

"Unofficially, all I can tell you is that James Lawless is Missing in Action. He's been missing for four years, Phoebe."

None of them spoke for a moment before the General came back in quietly. "If you give me some time, I'll go through channels. See what I can find out. In the meantime, Shane, I need you to submit an official inquiry to the Army on the sister's behalf. I'll get back to you guys as soon as I know more."

20

Sometimes life kicks you in the teeth. Kick back.

— Fiona O'Malley's Journal

Neither one of them spoke in the moments after the phone call. Shane blew out a breath, and Phoebe waited for him to break the silence.

"Wow."

"That's an understatement," she said.

Shane huffed. "Yeah. No kidding."

"Will you tell Laura right away?"

Shane shook his head, but it was the slow kind of shake that said there was more hesitation than decision in it. "I don't know. Depending on the circumstances, it's entirely possible missing in action might mean he's dead, but they were unable to recover a body."

"True." Phoebe's single word hung in the air.

"I can't get her hopes up only to find out..."

Phoebe nodded. "My dad won't make us wait any longer than necessary. If you want to prepare a letter on Laura's behalf, I can give you his direct fax to get it to Carson right away."

"Thank you."

Shane sat motionless in his chair as Phoebe stood and went to the door. His voice stopped her. "Phoebe."

"Yeah?" She turned and saw him watching her.

"Really, Phoebe. Thank you for that. For calling your dad. You just cut through what I'm sure would have been a lot of red tape. Even if this doesn't end with good news, knowing what happened to James will help Laura."

Phoebe swallowed and nodded before walking out. It felt good being able to help. She'd watched Shane help everyone in the town. They relied on him for so much. Being able to be a part of that, even if it was because of her father's influence, not her own, felt good. Especially where Laura was concerned. In only the few weeks Phoebe had known her, Laura had treated her as though they'd been friends for life.

21

Slow is every foot on an unknown path.

— IRISH PROVERB RECORDED IN FIONA O'MALLEY'S
JOURNAL

"Do you think there's any truth to it?" Garret asked the question Shane had been asking himself since Beverly's visit.

"I don't know. I wish I had the answer, but I really don't know."

Garret nodded. "The medical examiner is still running blood tests. I have to tell you, nothing at the scene seemed out of place." He rubbed at his forehead. "I did collect evidence at the scene, of course. I'm having that processed as well, but unfortunately, the labs are backed up as always."

Garret looked out the window of his office, jaw clenched, before turning back to Shane. "I'll find the answer, but it might take time."

Shane nodded. He should have left, but found himself stuck to his chair.

Garret turned and looked at him, a slow grin crossing his face.

"What?" Shane asked, sounding a little like the sullen teenager he'd once been.

"You want to ask me about Phoebe."

"Not true," said Shane, resisting the urge to cross his arms. "I want to ask you about Ashley."

Now Garret laughed. "But you're asking me about Ashley because you really want to know what you should do about Phoebe."

"I think you're violating all kinds of man codes right now. You're not supposed to laugh at a guy when he's down."

"Screw that. I'll laugh at you all I want. I'll still tell you what to do, but I'll laugh my ass off while I'm doing it."

"You done?" Shane asked.

"Yeah, yeah, I'm done. But you want to know if I had any qualms dating Ashley when she was involved in a case I was working?"

"Yeah."

"I had a lot of qualms about it, and technically, my partner and I cleared her before we dated. But, you have to ask yourself if this feels different. If she's just another girl or if you know this one might just go somewhere."

Shane didn't have to ask himself. He knew the answer to that without thinking. Phoebe was different from everyone he'd dated. He liked the way he felt when he was with her. When he wasn't with her, he was thinking about her. When she smiled or laughed, he felt like he'd won the lottery and he wanted to do it again.

It was a total cliché, but she lived up to her name. She brought him pure joy.

And when he'd kissed her? *That* had told him a lot. That one kiss had somehow been better than a hell of a lot of the sex he'd had in the past. He still hadn't figured out how the hell that was possible. Shit, they'd been fully clothed and in public.

Garret laughed again and Shane bit down on the urge to launch himself over the desk and strangle his friend.

"Yeah," Garret said. "There's your answer."

"I didn't say anything."

That just made Garret laugh harder.

"You're a dick," Shane said as he walked out of the office, but he was grinning.

22

Enough and no waste is as good as a feast.

— IRISH PROVERB RECORDED IN FIONA O'MALLEY'S
JOURNAL

"So, nobody in the town knows you guys do this?"
Phoebe's eyes lit with the excitement of someone
who'd been let in on a secret.

Shane watched her and thought about what he and
Garret had talked about. He wanted her. He'd decided that.
But he'd also figured out along the way that she wasn't sure
she wanted him. That left him with the challenge of trying
to figure out how to get her on board with his plan.

Would it be awful to make up excuses for them to work
late into the night together?

Shane shook the thought away. That had to qualify for
sexual harassment. Sometimes it sucked being a lawyer.
And a nice guy.

"Have dinner with me." The words came out of nowhere, but once they were out there, he realized it was the best move.

Or not. Her head shot up from where she'd been looking over the papers again. "What?"

He tugged the papers from her hand and set them down. "I was wrong. About the kiss. It wasn't a mistake. We're adults, and I like you. Clearly," he grinned, "you like me."

She smirked and he couldn't help but laugh. It had the effect he'd hoped for. It broke the tension between them that had been simmering all week.

He quieted. "I like you a lot, Phoebe. I think it's worth seeing where this goes. We can go to dinner a few times." He took hold of her hand, lightly so she could pull it away if she wanted to, before gripping more firmly. "We'll go to dinner, I'll kiss you a few more times, you'll like it. I promise." He was teasing her, and it was working.

Her teeth bit into her lip and she leaned toward him a fraction of an inch. It was enough.

Shane slipped one hand into her curls and tilted her face to his, but didn't kiss her. "We don't have to let it enter the office. If things don't work out, we'll go back to what we were. Two people who work really well together and respect the hell out of each other."

She looked at him a beat and he found himself holding his breath before she gave a small nod.

Shane felt a smile break slowly and build across his face. "Yeah?"

He inched closer and her breath hitched as she leaned in, closing the distance even more.

"Yeah," she breathed, and it was all he could do not to haul her closer and kiss her.

Shane slid his hands down her torso and, slowly, to her hips. Then, he did the opposite of what every muscle in his body ached to do. He put a foot of distance between them.

The stunned look on her face said she hadn't expected the move. That only made him smile more. He had a feeling keeping Phoebe Joy on her toes was a very good thing. Hard, but good.

"So, I'll pick you up in your office at six?"

She laughed. "No. Pick me up at my house at seven."

He made a mock grimace of pain and held his chest. "You're going to make me wait an extra hour?"

"I am," she tossed over her shoulder as she walked out the door.

23

I've found a dear place filled with dear friends. I could ask for nothing more.

— FIONA O'MALLEY'S JOURNAL

S hane thought about calling Ashley, but looked at the clock. If he remembered correctly, she usually took her afternoon break from the library about the same time each day.

"Margaret," he said as he walked through the lobby, "I'm going to run out for about an hour."

She nodded and waved, moving the stacks of cards on her online solitaire game. She took her break about this time each day, too.

Shane walked the three and a half blocks to the library, pulling open the front door to find Ashley coming out.

"Hey, I was just coming to see if I could catch you on your break."

"I'm not sure I'm talking to you." Ashley brushed past him and walked back out on the sidewalk.

Shane followed. "What did I do now?"

"It's what you're not doing." She hitched her bag further up on her shoulder and scowled at him, walking toward the community center.

"And what is that?"

"You haven't asked Phoebe out." Ashley stopped and turned to him, hands on hips. "Look, I get you're kind of chicken about it since you guys work together. I mean, yeah, dating your paralegal isn't the best idea, but let's face it, you're not getting any younger."

Shane laughed at that as she eyed him up and down like he was some kind of geriatric case instead of a guy in his thirties. "I'm not, huh?"

"No. You're really not." This was said with a shake of her head, as though her scan had come up wanting.

"And I assume you're going to tell me what to do?" It was in Ashley's makeup to tell everyone in town what to do. In fact, she knew everything about everyone. He was hoping that would help him.

"Yes. Ask Phoebe out. Anyone can see you guys are perfect for each other."

"Done."

She eyed him. "Really?"

Shane gave a nod. "I just asked her out. We're having dinner tonight."

"Huh." Ashley looked almost disappointed, like she'd been looking forward to badgering him into following her advice.

He grinned. "Sorry. I talked to Garret earlier and he convinced me."

"Oh. Well, I guess that's okay then."

"So, you're talking to me, then?"

"Yup. What can I do for you?"

Shane glanced around. They were standing on the sidewalk between the community center and the library.

"Were you going to the community center?" He asked.

"Yes." She glanced over her shoulder. "I was going to run by and see if Haddie needed me to pick anything up for her when I go to the store later."

"Why don't I go with you and we can talk after?"

She shrugged a response before walking toward the center again. Shane knew his request had come out of nowhere, but he wanted to see what the center was like. Fiona spent time there. Maybe getting a sense of where she spent her days would help him understand more about what Beverly had been talking about.

Even though he'd talked to Garret and he knew Garret would follow through, the conversation with Beverly had been weighing on him. She'd been right. As much as Shane believed it was possible Fiona had committed suicide because of the dementia she'd experienced, Fiona hadn't been depressed. She'd been a woman who, as far as he could see, had been continuing with her life despite what she'd experienced. The conflict was troubling him.

They walked into the front of the community center, which was primarily one large room. There were bathrooms and a few offices off to the right side, and a small kitchenette in a room at the end of the entrance hall. The rest was one large open area. One side held a variety of seating areas, couches and loveseats, as well as a few bistro style tables. Shane knew the kitchenette held a small automatic espresso machine because his office had been the one to donate it when the community center was looking for items during a remodel, two years before.

Up near the front windows of the community center was a bank of computers where visitors could log on or attend classes offered throughout the month. The back corner of the room was a large open area where they held exercise classes, art classes, and other programs every day. From what he'd heard, they'd been doing a lot to pull in young people to work with the seniors. They started a tutoring program where the seniors tutored kids from the local schools, and they'd enlisted teenagers to come in and teach some of the classes to the seniors.

There was a chorus of hellos for Ashley when she entered the room. It didn't surprise Shane at all. Ashley was a little bit like the town's daughter. She had come here as a teenager when the Walkers adopted her after leaving several hellish foster placements. Although Ashley's love for the Walkers had always been clear, she was a bit of a wild child. She made high school interesting, to say the least.

But she'd grown into someone the town could be—and was—proud of. She was the local librarian, but also friends to just about everyone and anyone who needed her. When she'd married Garret last year, and he'd taken over as chief of police, it had only solidified her position in town.

They made their way over to the computer area, where

Haddie sat in front of one of the computers practically giggling with the woman next to her.

"Haddie," Ashley said in the way one might talk to the kind of teenager Ashley had been. "I have a feeling that whatever you're up to, it isn't anything good."

The white-haired woman spun in her seat to face Ashley and Shane, a broad smile firmly in place. "You know it. We're working on hacking the system so we can get porn on the center computers. They have some silly filter on here like we're not all adults."

"Eeeeew." Ashley's comment echoed what was happening in Shane's head, but he was beyond words. The word "porn" coming out of Haddie's mouth had stopped him in his tracks.

"We might be old, but were not dead yet." Haddie laughed, but stopped when she saw Miriam, the director of the center standing frozen in place a few feet away. Miriam looked positively stricken.

"I'm sorry, Miriam." Haddie did sound sorry and Miriam nodded, her gaze flicking over all of them before walking away.

Haddie and the woman sitting next to her shared a guilty look. "Miriam has taken Fiona's death pretty hard. Most of us here tend to..." Haddie looked up as though thinking, "well, we tend to be a little more pragmatic about death. None of us are so far away from it anymore, and I guess we know that, so it's become all the more important for us to focus on the here and now."

"Was Miriam close to Fiona?" Shane asked the question, knowing Fiona had mentioned Miriam to him a few times in their conversations. Fiona loved coming to the senior center, and seemed to like Miriam, from what he could tell. He wanted to know Haddie's take on things, though.

Another woman called Haddie's friend away from the computer bank and she wandered off to join their conversation before Haddie answered.

"They were no closer than Miriam is close to all of us. She makes a point to get to know everyone, and takes good care of all of us here. She makes batches of teas for some of us. Medicinal stuff she says will help with aches and pains and whatnot. Knows which of us can have sugar in our cocoa and who needs that damned fake sweetener."

Shane saw Ashley raised a brow to Haddie and Haddie scowled her way. "Don't worry, she gives me the damned fake shit. Anyway, she bakes for us and dotes on everyone, but I think Miriam is taking Fiona's death hard because Fiona killed herself. It seems like Miriam is having a hard time handling that."

Haddie's eyes crossed to where Miriam now floated among people working on paintings and sketches in an art class. "I have a feeling she's taking it as a blow that Fiona wouldn't have come to her or that she somehow didn't see it coming." Haddie looked up at them and shook her head. "Or I could be wrong. What do I know?"

Ashley sat in the computer chair vacated by the other woman, and took Haddie's hand in hers. "I don't know, you always seem to read people pretty damned well if you ask me."

"Well, this was one that none of us read. I don't think any of us saw Fiona doing this."

Shane sat in the chair on the other side of Haddie, unable to pass up the chance to ask her about Fiona. He was beginning to feel like he'd really screwed up, telling Garrett Fiona might have killed herself. Why had he been so quick to believe that if others weren't? "She didn't seem depressed about anything to you?"

Haddie swiveled his way. "No, but I don't know if she would have confided in me. We were friends, but she was closest to Beverly. And, of course, Elliot."

Shane knew Ashley was looking at him funny, probably wondering why he was so interested. He'd have to explain it to her after they left. "Did you know she was having some symptoms of dementia?"

Haddie's eyes went round. "No, she didn't tell me. And I never saw anything that made me think she might." She looked back at Ashley. "Poor Elliot has been beside himself. He's still not back at work. A few of us went by to visit him and I don't think he's even getting himself up and dressed every day. Beverly said she would go by and check on him and see if she could get him back out into the world."

Haddie took a deep breath as though ridding herself of the depressing conversation, and turned bright eyes to Ashley. "Now, tell me what you're doing here on your break. I thought we talked about you not spending all your time with old biddies."

Ashley laughed. "Hey, I happen to like old biddies. Besides, you know as well as anyone, I spend plenty of time with young biddies, too."

Shane knew she meant the circle of Cora, Laura, Katelyn, and now he supposed Phoebe as well.

"But I really came by to see if you needed me to get you anything at the store. I'm going to run over this afternoon and I can drop things off at your house if you'd like."

"Oh, you're a dear." Haddie patted Ashley's hand, but looked over at Shane. "This is really her way of trying to control my blood sugar better. She doesn't trust me to do it on my own."

"Not true." Ashley was laughing as she said it.

"In that case, get me some real ice cream and some real cookies."

The two women said the next line together: "not the kind with that damned fake sugar."

Ashley sighed and shook her head at Haddie. "Maybe a little."

Ashley and Shane walked out, greeted by the sun and heat of the ninety-eight-degree day. Shane could see why so many of the town's elderly spent time at the center. Not only was it a chance to socialize and keep active, it had central air and rows of ceiling fans to keep the air moving. If he had to guess, he'd bet many of the people who spent their days there couldn't afford to cool their houses to that level in the Texas heat.

"Okay, do you want to tell me what's going on or are we going to play more games?" Ashley was giving him the kind of look that said she didn't plan to play anymore.

Shane pulled her along toward the back parking lot of the library where he knew she would be parked. "Drive me back to the office and I'll fill you in on the way." This wasn't a conversation he wanted anyone overhearing.

They slid into her car and she started it up. "Beverly

came to see me. She's not convinced Fiona committed suicide."

Ashley's eyes went wide, but she didn't comment.

"I'm not sure one way or the other, but what she said made a lot of sense. Fiona was planning vacations and things. I knew she was having some dementia issues but when Bev really made me sit down and think about it, I realized she was concerned about the symptoms, but not depressed. Plus, she hadn't been to see Dr. Allen yet, so she didn't know for sure what was going on."

"Please tell me you talked to Garret about this."

"I did." Shane nodded. "He's going to look into it, and I trust him." She raised a brow at this. "I do. But, it's been eating at me. I wanted to talk to people a little, see what Fiona had been doing. Maybe just hear for myself what other people thought without spreading it around town."

Ashley nodded. He didn't need to ask her not to tell people. He knew she wouldn't. If anything, Ashley Hensley was too good at keeping secrets. She'd kept some heavy secrets about her own life for a long time.

"I didn't know Fiona well, but I did see her when I went to pick Haddie up at the center." No one in town ever questioned why Ashley and Haddie were so close. The two women were so alike, it was almost comical. They might not be related, but Ashley cared for Haddie as someone might care for a grandparent. "She didn't strike me as someone who was depressed, but when I heard about her suicide, I just thought there must have been something going on we didn't know about. Something medical or whatever that the town hadn't heard about. Or maybe something with her and Elliot."

She pulled the car up in front of the law office but Shane didn't move to get out. "He's wrecked. I need to go by and check on him, but Bev said he's holed up in the house and isn't handling things well at all."

"I don't blame him." Ashley shook her head and he could see her staving off emotion. "I think I'd be in bed for months if anything..."

She didn't finish but Shane understood. His eyes moved to the law office window. He couldn't see her but Phoebe was in there. What he felt for Phoebe couldn't begin to compare to what Garret and Ashley had, but he wanted what they had. Wanted that connection, the love, the family. That sense of being complete because you found the one person you were meant to be with. Phoebe was the first woman in a long time who'd made him feel like that might be possible.

Ashley didn't miss a beat. "You're taking her someplace nice, I hope?"

Shane turned and grinned. "I'm not reviewing a detailed plan of my date with you, Ash."

"You should." Her smirk was one of the reasons he liked hanging out with her. She was never afraid to speak her mind. "I know what I'm doing. I'm an expert, remember?"

Shane tipped back his head and laughed. Ashley's sister had revealed Ashley's secret identity as a romance novelist, spilling her pen name to all of Evers, last year. Ashley, it turned out, had been writing romantic suspense novels under a pen name for a year or two, and doing it quite well, it turned out. She'd hit several of the bestseller lists and had a real following.

Shane reached for the door handle. "Noted. If I run into trouble, I'll give you a call."

She shrugged. "You should."

Shane gave her one more smiling shake of his head—an action that happened a lot around this particular friend—and headed into the office. He hadn't gotten much more information than he'd had on Fiona when he left, but from what he'd heard, he was glad Beverly had come to him. He felt better knowing Garret was going to be looking more closely at Fiona's death. If nothing else, maybe it would bring them all some much-needed closure.

24

If I could give one thing to my family and my friends, it would be that they love themselves. That they know that they are always *enough.*

— FIONA O'MALLEY'S JOURNAL

Phoebe should have asked for three hours between work and their date. She hadn't been this nervous for a date in a long time. A lot of her relationships had just formed as she hung out with groups of her friends. There hadn't always been a formal start to them like this. How sad was that for a twenty-nine-year-old?

She looked down at the clothes strewn over her bed and the chair in the corner of her room. How cliché was that? She had no idea what to wear.

She tugged at the dress she had on. It was a casual sundress that could work for a pizza place or something a little fancier. She doubted Shane planned to take her someplace that would require something super dressed up. Just in case, she slid off the sandals she wore and put on a pair that had sparkly gemstones edging the straps. With this addition, the dress could work for anywhere.

There, she thought, with a nod in the mirror. Unless it was too short. She spun to look at the dress from the back. It fell to mid-thigh. It definitely wasn't prudish, but she wasn't entirely sure if it went too far in the other direction. Had she hit hussy-ville?

She pulled up Facetime and dialed Chelsea.

"Hey girl, what's up?" Chelsea didn't seem to think it was odd for Phoebe to Facetime her.

"I need help." Phoebe turned her back to the mirror and held her phone up high, hoping Chelsea could see the back of her dress in the mirror.

"Hot." Chelsea's answer was immediate. "Oh! You have a date, don't you? Who is it?"

Phoebe didn't reply. "So, it's not too trashy? I feel like it's a little short."

Chelsea made a dismissive sound. "No. It's not. It's got tiny baby blue flowers all over it. How could that be trashy? You'd need to lose another two inches to hit trash level. Now, tell me who is the date with? Have I met him?"

Phoebe brought the phone back down to her face and talked as she ran into the bathroom for one more check of her hair and makeup. She wasn't looking forward to this part of the conversation.

"It's Shane."

"Your boss, Shane? That Shane?"

Phoebe sighed. "That Shane. I'm sorry, Chelsea, I know

you don't think it's a good idea, but, well...I just feel like I need to see where it's going to go. If I end up with my heart crushed and out of a job, so be it."

"Pheebs," Chelsea's sigh was probably heavier than it needed to be. She always did love her drama, but Phoebe didn't really want that drama aimed at her. "I just don't want to see you go down this path again."

Phoebe took a breath and glanced at the clock. Two minutes to seven. "Listen, I know you mean well, Chelsea, but I'm not really sure I've been down *this* road before. I know you think you see a pattern here, and maybe you're right. I did date some guys in the past who were lame and headed nowhere, and yes, I should have been able to see they weren't headed in the same direction as me. This is different. Shane isn't like them."

Chelsea looked a bit taken aback that Phoebe might argue with her, but she was going to need to get over that. Phoebe wasn't going to live her life based on what her friend said she should do. Friends should give input and advice and comfort, but they should also be willing to stand by you if you didn't take that advice or follow every plan they came up with for your life. Shouldn't they?

"Okay, then. Well, have a good time on your date."

The call disconnected and Phoebe stared at the phone for a minute, feeling both annoyed and dismayed. She didn't want to fight with Chelsea. But that didn't mean she didn't want to see where this might go with Shane.

She looked down at the hem of her skirt again, debating another change when she heard a knock on the door. Looked like this dress was going to have to do.

Phoebe pulled open the door to her apartment and froze.

Shane had apparently gone home, too.

Her breath seemed to be stuck in her chest as she looked at him. His hair was still a little damp from his shower and it was all Phoebe could do not to choke as unbidden images of him standing under a sluice of hot water flooded her brain. He wore a casual Henley shirt and jeans.

Correction. They should have been casual. On him, they were anything but. The navy fabric of the shirt stretched over muscles she wanted to rub up against, and the jeans. Well, the jeans just plain made her mouth water.

"Wow, Phoebe." He seemed to breathe the words, and Phoebe peeled her eyes from his muscles to smile at him.

"Right back atchya, lawyerman."

He rewarded her with one of those laughs she'd begun to crave. The one where he tipped his head back and laughed fully, easily. He could be so serious behind his desk at work. She liked seeing him this way.

He reached for her hand. "Ready?"

Phoebe nodded and pulled the door shut behind her. It was really all she could do. The minute his large hand had taken hold of hers, she'd all but melted into a puddle on the floor. It felt so good to walk with him down the steps to his waiting car.

Shane looked back up toward her apartment. "You really lucked out with this apartment. I think Mrs. Sassan's son was living up here for four or five years. You happened to move to town right when she decided he needed to grow up."

"Oh, I know." Phoebe smiled as he opened the door for her and she slid into the leather seat of the Jaguar. A giggle escaped her as she thought again that she was really happy with her choice of his car. Luckily for her, Shane missed it as he jogged to his side of the car and slid in. "Mrs. Sassan treated me to the whole story about her good-for-nothing lazy offspring, as she calls him. By the end of it, I didn't know whether to pity Matt or dislike him. He can't really be as bad as she says he is, can he?"

"Oh, he is. He's basically lived off of her since we all graduated years ago. He bartends, but spends most of the money he earns on toys and stuff. Old cars that used to fill her driveway. He really needed to be kicked out. He needs to grow up."

"You sound so stern," she said, looking at his profile as he drove.

Shane laughed. "Do you mean I sound like a stick-in-the-mud? That's what my brother is always telling me."

Phoebe shrugged her shoulder. "You seem like someone who knows what they want in life. And like someone who doesn't want to let other people down or be a burden to people."

"Responsible," Shane said, and now he didn't look overly comfortable with the label.

Phoebe studied him a bit longer. "Yes," she said slowly. "But you're also fun and kind."

He shot her an oh-thanks-for-the-compliments kind of look and she lowered her tone. "And sexy as hell. There's something to be said about wanting to get you to unbutton your shirt or loosen your tie. Trust me, the buttoned-up look isn't a bad one on you."

The car swerved a hair before Shane corrected, shooting her a glance. "I can't tell if you're joking or not."

Phoebe laughed. "I'm really not." She was a little surprised at how up front and bold she was being, but he seemed to bring it out in her. She didn't feel uncomfortable telling him what he did to her. "You make me itch to make you lose control. It's a good thing. Trust me."

Shane was silent for a minute but she could feel him glancing at her as he drove.

She turned in her seat and met his gaze full on. "Focus on the road, Shane," she said her voice soft and seductive, loving the look that lit his eyes when she did.

"Christ, you'll be the death of me, woman."

"Where are you taking me?"

"Maybe back to my place if you keep this up."

Now it was Phoebe's turn to laugh that full, real laugh. "On a first date, Shane?"

He shook his head at her. "No, not on a first date." There was promise in those words and she felt that promise right through to her toes. "If you don't mind a bit of a drive, I'm taking you to August E's out in Fredericksburg. They have an amazing view and we should make it in time for sunset."

Their conversation on the road was light and easy, but Phoebe felt the thrum of excitement deep in her belly that came from a new relationship. The nice thing with Shane, though, was that she didn't feel overly nervous with him the way she sometimes had with other men. He had this way of setting her at ease and exciting her all at once.

Shane took her hand in his as they walked toward the restaurant. The interior was modern and sleek, but when they were led to the back deck, the atmosphere was more rustic and casual. And Shane had been right, the view was beautiful as the sun began to set in the sky.

It was the kind of restaurant where several wait staff approached. One bringing bread and another offering sparkling or still water. One more approached to tell them the specials and take their drink order.

When their orders had been placed and they were alone, Shane sat back in his chair. "So, tell me about the General."

Phoebe laughed. "I don't usually tell my friends about him. I mean, of course, growing up on military bases, everyone knew who my dad was, but once I moved out on my own, it was a detail I kept to myself."

Shane sipped his water. "It can be a little intimidating, I'd imagine."

"Ya think?" Phoebe laughed. She knew her dad was intimidating. "Wait until you meet him. He's larger than life and loves to do that thing where he just stares people down waiting for them to talk, even if the only question on the table is what they had for breakfast."

"That must have made dating fun."

She rolled her eyes. "You have no idea. No one wanted to touch me with a ten-foot pole when I was in high school."

Shane grinned at her. "Something tells me you had dates whether your dad approved or not. Something also tells me his staring trick doesn't work on you."

Phoebe pointed at him. "So true. Not the date thing,

although I guess I did, but the staring trick. Much to his dismay, I learned to sit still and wait him out by the time I was twelve or thirteen. We'd have these epic staring contests." She scrunched up her nose. "No, they were more like battles. Epic staring battles."

"Who'd win in the end?"

"Neither. My dad is also maddeningly adept at negotiating truces. He'd come in my room and talk me out of whatever pout I was in and we'd come to some compromise. He was good at making me feel like I'd gotten something out of him, even though he always won the war." She smiled with the memories. "He's a great dad. Of course, if you ask him, he'd say he spoiled me rotten."

They paused for a minute while their salads were served and Phoebe took a bite of pear with gorgonzola cheese.

"Do you see your mom at all?" Shane asked.

Phoebe finished her bite and swallowed, not without some effort. Any talk of her dad always led to talk of her mom, and that was the part of the conversation she hated. Her mother had left her when she was only weeks old. During her kinder, gentler moments, Phoebe had wondered if postpartum depression might have played a part in her mother's decision. But the more she knew about her mom, the less likely that seemed.

"They were an odd match right from the start. My dad kept a little box of things from my mom for me to look through when I was older. She was all lovey-dovey hippie child, hence my name."

"I happen to like your name."

Now Phoebe rolled her eyes at him. "Anyway, she was all

in to being free, not wanting to lock herself into marriage. She was much younger than my dad. I think she thought she could just take a baby on the road with her and her band and raise me as more of a friend than a child. That's the sense I always got, anyway."

Shane didn't offer the normal platitudes and pity she was used to at the end of the story. "Have you ever looked for her?"

Phoebe nodded. "When I was 20. I looked her up and found her living in a small town in Maine. She has no kids, but it looks like she runs a small art gallery in a coastal town."

"Do you think you might ever go see her?" Shane asked as he picked up his beer glass.

"I tried to get in touch." Phoebe tasted her wine, and murmured her approval. It was crisp and light, and it helped clear away the lump in her throat that had developed with talking about her mom. "I wrote to her after I found her, but she didn't respond."

"I've done a bang-up job keeping this conversation cheerful."

Phoebe couldn't help but laugh at the wry comment.

"Okay, your turn. Tell me all about your childhood."

"Ah, my childhood. Well, when you combine the uncertainty of running a ranch with a father who would rather play around with inventions in the barn than house animals there, you get my childhood."

"Inventions?"

"Everything from tools to glue. It was the glue that

ended up striking gold. And it turns out he wasn't even aiming for glue."

Phoebe was about to cut into the chicken that had been put where her salad plate had been moments before, but she looked up at that. "What was he going for?"

"No one really knows for sure, and he liked to be mysterious about it, but he ended up with two industrial glues that are used in all kinds of applications. Chances are it's on at least one or two things in your apartment right now. He has a few smaller patents on some other items that paid off, but those are the big ones."

She eyed him. "But those didn't happen until you were older, did they?"

"No, not until after years of watching my mom cover for him. She still can't see it. As far as she's concerned, he was a great dad and a wonderful man."

"He wasn't?"

Shane looked at his drink for a minute. "I sound like an ass, I think, whenever I talk about him. He was a great dad, in some ways. I never doubted I was loved, and that means a lot. I guess, when it really comes down to it, that's the most important thing. But there were times that I had to watch my mom scrape together the money for things we needed and I always hated that. I hated to see how much she would worry. She would hide it from him, but as soon as he left the house I could see the strain on her."

"It makes sense." At his puzzled look, she explained. "You seem to take everything on your shoulders. You take care of everyone, trying to make sure you know what everybody needs before they even know they need it. I would bet that came from trying to take care of your mom when you were younger."

Shane nodded. "You're probably right. As soon as I could, I got a job unloading pallets and stocking shelves down at the feed store. When I was older, I added a second job. Anything I could do, to take away from the pressure my mom had to deal with."

"And after you guys made your millions, you started providing grants to people in the town?" Phoebe thought back to the grant papers she had reviewed for him that morning, and smiled at the memory of him taking them out of her hands to ask her on a date. Phoebe didn't know for sure that the family had millions, but she would guess based on the number of grants she'd seen them give people around the town, their pockets were fairly deep.

"Yep. The first one we started with was the feed store. Tom Jansen had helped me by giving me my first job, and was always good to me and my family. He needed money to expand the store so we set up our first grant."

"And no one in the town knows where they're coming from?" Phoebe shook her head, not sure that was possible. Surely the town knew the family had come into money.

"I'm sure people suspect." Shane shrugged. "But Ashley covers for us. She keeps helping people pour through guides to different grants around the country. Once she knows what someone is looking for, she lets us know. Then we're able to slip a grant designed for that person into the pile of options she pulls for them. They never need to know the grant wasn't actually one that was open to other people.

They simply fill out a form and we set them up with what they need."

"That's..." Phoebe searched for the right words, but came up wanting. "It's incredible. Giving something without any expectation of credit or gratitude."

Shane lifted a shoulder. "We get to watch their businesses survive or grow, and we get to see people finish school or give their children something they needed. We do a few things in our name. We gave some gifts to the school in dad's name. We donated to the new tourism board the town is putting together to increase tourism for local businesses. Things like that."

She could see the attention made him uncomfortable and had a feeling the whole family would be that way.

Phoebe pushed back her plate, stuffed, even though she was tempted to eat more. It all tasted delicious.

"How was the chicken?" Shane nodded to her plate.

"It was perfect. I just can't eat another bite. Unless it's dessert," she rushed to say. "I can always eat dessert."

Shane grinned at her and her stomach did that flip-flop again. "Good to know." He pushed back his plate and sat back.

The wait staff was swift, moving in to clear their plates and brush the crumbs from the table.

When they brought the dessert menu, Phoebe didn't know which one to choose.

"Tell me which ones you're thinking about." Shane had a wicked glint in his eye.

"The chocolate cake or the tres leches."

Shane turned to the waiter. "We'll take one each of those, please."

Phoebe groaned. "I won't be able to walk out of here."

Shane winked. "I'll carry you."

Phoebe blushed at the thought of him lifting her in his arms. Then her mind started to wander to all the places he could take her, and what he could do with her there.

He leaned across the table and took her hand, pulling her in closer. "I think I want to know where your head just went." His voice had lowered an octave and she had a feeling he knew exactly where her head had gone.

Phoebe glanced up to make sure nobody was standing nearby. "Sorry," she whispered, "I was just thinking about you carrying me away and, um..."

Shane made a sound that only a man can make, the kind that sent even more thoughts flashing through the Phoebe's mind. "I think I like where you're headed with that. And I'm not sure I can stick around for dessert anymore."

Phoebe gasped. "Bite your tongue. We never skip dessert."

Shane laughed and pulled back. "I did promise not to take you back to my place on the first date. I'm planning to stick with that."

Phoebe found herself nodding but on the inside, she was battling between disappointment and a sense of pleasure that he wanted to wait. She hadn't been so attracted to anyone in a long time, but the fact that he wanted to wait, that he didn't want to rush things between them, made this all the more appealing.

25

If you can find a way to be there for friends and family when
they need you, even with only a word or a quiet presence, do it.

— FIONA O'MALLEY'S JOURNAL

I t killed Shane to take Phoebe home at the end of the
night, but he knew it was the right thing to do. He didn't
want to sleep with her until he was sure this was headed
somewhere. If they went on a few dates and weren't feeling
as strongly about each other as they did now, they could
walk away and stay friends. But Shane knew once he took
Phoebe to bed, walking away and staying friends or continuing to work together probably wasn't going to happen.

He pulled up to the curb outside her apartment. She had
been lucky to rent the small studio over a garage in a quiet
neighborhood not far from downtown. The houses weren't
extravagant and they were close together, but the neighborhood was well kept up.

Shane opened Phoebe's car door and lifted her hand to tug her out. As she stepped to him, he pulled her in, loving the feel of her body in that light sundress against his. She was so soft, her breasts skimming across his chest. He threaded one hand through her hair and dipped to her mouth to taste her.

She was sweetness and spice all at once, and the combination was heady and sinful.

Shane would have liked to lose himself in her, but movement from the shadows near her steps had him breaking the kiss and moving her behind him. Shane turned to face the shadow, his blood pressure kicking up at the thought that Phoebe might be in danger.

"Get back in the car, Phoebe. Lock the doors," he said quietly.

He heard a gruff voice before the shadowed form came forward and took shape. "Watch where you're putting your hands, son. That's my daughter you're groping."

"Dad?" As Phoebe's voice came from behind him, Shane processed that he was facing General Brophy. Facing General Brophy with the taste and feel of the man's daughter much too fresh in his mind. Talk about killing the mood.

"Dad!" Now Phoebe shot around Shane and leapt at the large man standing there. The large man who was somehow both grinning at her and scowling at Shane at the same time. Phoebe had her arms wrapped around her father and the General held her with one arm as if the move took no effort. Something about it struck Shane. She was truly her daddy's girl.

It was suddenly very important to Shane that Phoebe's dad like him.

He waited as Phoebe and the General hugged before shaking the hand he offered Shane.

"Stop scowling, dad," Phoebe said after introducing them. "Come on, did you see how fast Shane put himself between you and me when he saw you step toward us in the dark?"

Shane almost laughed at her as she put all her energy into convincing her father of his chivalrous ways.

Her dad grumbled what seemed to be a grudging admission that he'd been impressed.

"What are you doing here?" Phoebe looped one arm into her father's arm and one into Shane's, leading the men on either side of her toward her apartment.

"Actually," the General said, "It's good that you're both here. I came to tell you in person what I found out about your friend's brother."

Shane felt his chest tighten. That didn't sound good. He felt like he was walking on leaden feet as they broke apart and took the outside flight of stairs that lead to Phoebe's apartment single file.

"What did you find out about James?" Phoebe asked as soon as they entered. She led the way to the couch and sat. It wasn't lost on Shane that her father took the seat beside her, leaving Shane to sit in the chair beside them. He almost didn't care. As much as he wanted to be close to Phoebe, his mind was fully focused on the whereabouts of Laura's brother at the moment.

"On the record, all I'm able to tell you is that James was

part of a unit running an op in South America in an area heavily controlled by guerrilla organizations. In fact, the specific groups at play there have changed hands a few times in the last few years."

Shane didn't like where this was headed.

The General continued and Shane wondered how many times he'd had to give a report like this to family members of the men who'd fought for him over the years. "His unit was under fire, sustaining heavy casualties. When they were able to get air support and another team in there to pull those guys out, there was no sign of James. The two surviving members of the unit swore they saw him sustain injuries he couldn't have survived, but there was no body, no signs of his remains."

Shane got the sense the General was trying to tone it down for Phoebe's sake, but she still looked pale. Shane stood and went to her side of the couch, sitting on the arm and taking her hand in his. She smiled up at him before looking back to her father.

"James is officially listed as missing-in-action. The two surviving members have pushed for a unit to go in again and try to bring his remains home, but the area is still a hotbed. It's controlled by violent drug cartels, guerrilla groups, and gun runners."

He paused and Shane jumped in. "You said this was what you could tell us on the record? What is the off-the-record piece of things?"

The General paused like he was assessing Phoebe, but then continued. "Off the record, there have been reports in the region of a man being held by one of the organizations in the area. They call him the Illusion and he certainly appears to be more myth and legend than truth. Local people say he has died many times, but that is taken by others to mean he has come close to death and survived. It's said he was captured and taken to the mountains and given over to a village of women to care for. No one expected him to live. They say he escaped for a time and was smuggling information out to government forces from within several of the guerrilla strongholds before he was recaptured and near death again."

"And you think this could be James?" Shane asked.

The General shook his head. "I don't even know if this man truly exists. The surviving members of James's unit have gathered intelligence on this Illusion. They've talked to people from the region and they believe he fits the description." He shook his head again. "Honestly, I don't know if it's them wanting their friend to be alive so badly they're willing to see it in anything or what. But it bothers me that the evac team wasn't able to find his body."

"What can we do?" Phoebe asked, echoing Shane's own questions racing around his head. He knew once he told Cade there was a chance James could be alive, it was very likely Cade would want to charter a plane and go to the area himself.

The General sighed. "I don't honestly know if there is anything you can do, but I'll tell you this. You said this woman, your friend, was the former Laura Kensington. She has political connections?"

Shane nodded, seeing where he was going with this. "Her father-in-law and his father before him were both

Senators. Her husband was the next in line, everyone thought, before he died."

"I can apply some pressure on my side of things, at least get the Army to investigate the stories, see if there's any truth to this. If we have a man in there who's being held, we need to know about it. If she can get her family to apply pressure from the outside, we might be able to open the file."

Shane rubbed a hand down his face. How could he tell Laura any of this? Knowing there was a possibility her brother was alive would kill her. And if the news didn't shred her, having to go to her former mother-in-law for this kind of favor might just finish the job.

26

Life is a strange lad.

— IRISH PROVERB RECORDED IN FIONA O'MALLEY'S
JOURNAL

S hane had arranged for them to have breakfast out at the ranch the following day. He was grateful to have Phoebe with him as they trudged up the steps to the porch. The General had offered to come, but Shane thought it would be best letting Laura hear the news with family and friends first. He could bring her to see the General later if she wanted to talk to him. He had no idea how Laura was going to take this news.

There were the usual hugs and kisses, as though they all hadn't seen each other in months or years instead of days, but Shane never minded. It felt good to be enveloped by family. Laura and Cade's daughter, Jamie, wrapped her small arms around Shane's neck and he breathed in the scent of the small child. The girl acted so much like Cade, mimicking all his mannerisms and his way with the animals, it was hard to remember at times that biologically, she belonged to Laura's late husband.

Josh Samuels, his mother's live-in boyfriend, carried hot oatmeal muffins to the table. "So, what is it that couldn't wait until dinner tomorrow?"

The family had a standard Sunday dinner that Shane had once again been able to attend, thanks to Phoebe getting him caught up on his workload.

Shane cleared his throat. "It's about your brother, Laura," he said, meeting his sister-in-law's gaze. He'd been more than a bit of an ass when Laura had shown up on the ranch two years back. She'd been running from her late husband's family, believing they wanted to take her child from her. Her mother-in-law had tried, for a time. Now, they lived in a shaky truce after her mother-in-law had moved to town.

Phoebe stood and reached a hand toward Jamie. "Any chance you could show me the puppies this morning? I've been dying to see them again."

Josh rose as well. "I'll go with you guys. The puppies are growing so quickly, they might be able to take the two of you down to the ground and lick you to death." He scooped Jamie up in his arms as she giggled at the image of puppies licking her and Phoebe, and the three left the room. The quiet of their absence made the silent stares all the more evident.

Cade broke the silence. "Have you found his grave?"

Shane shook his head, no. For more than a year now,

he'd been searching for the site of James's burial, hoping to give Laura the chance to say good-bye.

"Laura," Shane began, "Phoebe was finally able to help me piece things together and track down what happened to James. It turns out, James entered the Army after you left your father's home."

Laura's eyes turned soft at the news and he thought she might cry, but she kept the tears at bay throughout the whole story. He told her of Phoebe's outreach to the General and what the General had shared with them the night before.

"If it's okay with you, Laura, I'd like to go see Martha Kensington for you. To ask her to apply pressure and see if we can get the Army to investigate the rumors. I'm sure she has contacts she can call."

"And if she doesn't," Cade said, arms wrapped around Laura, holding her tight to him, "I'll go down there myself or hire people to go in for us."

Laura turned stunned eyes to him. "No, you won't Cade Bishop. You can hire all the men you want, but I won't watch you walk into a war zone, even for my brother. It took me years to find you. You're the father of my child and the man I plan to spend a good long life with. I need you here and alive to do that."

She held her hand at the base of her neck, as though breathing through the idea of Cade trying to find her brother was difficult.

Shane cut in. "Let's talk to Martha first and see if she can get the Army to do this. They know the area, the players. If not, I think the General might be able to connect us with the right people to send into the region. Hell, right now, I don't even know exactly where he is, and we don't know for sure that he's..." He didn't finish the thought. They all knew what he meant.

"I'll go see Martha." Laura looked to Shane as she said this.

"Are you sure? I can take care of it for you," Shane said.

"No, it's all right. She's been seeing Jamie these last few months. We meet at the park every other week. When she's old enough, I'll explain who Martha is to Jamie and why she's in her life." She gripped Cade's hand. "She'll help."

Shane nodded. He knew it would kill Laura to ask the woman for help. Laura had lived for three years in a marriage where she was brutally battered. It would have been impossible for Martha Kensington not to know what was happening. The woman had never once lifted a finger to stop her son.

Laura had once told Shane she thought Martha had probably been subjected to something similar when her husband was alive, but Cade and Shane were both less forgiving than Laura. Still, if she could help them find out if James was alive and get him out of whatever hellhole he was in, it would go a long way toward making up for what she'd done to Laura for all those years.

May stood, leaning heavily on her cane. "Shane, let's go on down to the barn and let Laura and Cade have a few minutes to absorb this. You can tell me all about Phoebe on the way down."

They stopped on the porch to trade out May's cane for the wheelchair she used out on the ranch. Theirs was probably the only ranch in Texas with paved wheelchair access paths and ramps between the house and all the barns and out buildings.

As Shane pushed her toward the barn that held the rescued animals Cade worked with, May opened her interrogation. "Phoebe makes you very happy. I can see it, even when you're here to deliver news like this."

Shane didn't answer, but he was smiling, nonetheless.

His mother let out a snort. "And, heaven knows she's better than those vacuous empty-headed women you usually have on your arm."

"Ma!" May Bishop was always kind. Always.

"Well, it's true. And you need to hear it. You've had this notion that your wife needs to fit some set of criteria like a little checklist in your head. It's about time you threw that damned checklist out."

Shane couldn't help but think that Phoebe matched every check on his list. His new list, anyway. She was sexy as hell, but she was also smart and funny and she made him laugh. She made him want things for different reasons than he'd wanted them before.

In the past, wanting a wife and family had been something he just thought he needed to do. Maybe it had been some part of wanting to prove he could do it better than his dad. That he could support them and give them whatever they needed.

Phoebe made him see family for what it would be with her. It would be about coming together, putting their best selves into their children. As they approached the barn, Phoebe came out carrying Jamie with Josh by her side making faces at the little girl. Phoebe laughed, that free laugh she always had. The one that said it came from her heart, her soul. The one that filled his heart and soul each time he heard it.

He had planned to take things slow with her. To make sure this didn't go too far, too fast, in case they wanted to back out. In case they decided they needed to go back to just working together.

Looking at her now, he knew that was hopeless. It had already gone past the point of no return for him. He only hoped she was on the same page as he was.

27

Pity him who makes an opinion certainty.

— IRISH PROVERB RECORDED IN FIONA O'MALLEY'S
JOURNAL

Shane was going to have to wait through the weekend to see if Phoebe was on the same page as he was. Her dad stayed in town for the weekend, taking up most of her time. Shane joined them for dinner on Saturday evening, but keeping his distance during the meal had been hard. No leaning over to the table to brush a quick kiss over her lips, no hands running up and down her arm or leg at the table. And there definitely wasn't any talk of what she felt for him.

For the first time in memory, dinner at his mother's house on Sunday was a little subdued. They all laughed and talked about how cute Jamie was in her new cowboy hat, but Shane could see the strain on Laura's face as they began the long wait for news of her brother.

And if Shane were honest, he was missing having Phoebe there with him, which was stupid since she'd only accompanied him twice before.

He was on his way back from dinner when his phone rang. He hit the car's Bluetooth button and answered, hearing Garret's voice in reply.

"Hey Shane, do you have time to talk this evening? Maybe I can swing by your place if you're headed home?"

"Sure. I can meet you there in twenty minutes?"

"You got it."

Just shy of twenty minutes later, he pulled up to his place, seeing Garret waiting for him in his car.

"Hey, I thought you had your deputies covering most weekends so you could have some time with Ashley?" Shane unlocked his door and let them in, tossing the keys on the small shelf by the door. Garret was in uniform, so he didn't bother to offer him a beer.

Instead, he poured two glasses of water and led the way to the living room at the back of his apartment.

Garret answered as they settled into the large recliners that sat in front of the television. Not that Shane used the space much anymore, but at one point, watching baseball and hockey in the room had been one of the ways he unwound.

"I usually do, but the medical examiner let me know he faxed the results of the autopsy over to my office late last night. I wanted to get on it right away."

"Did he find anything?"

"Yeah." Garret's expression was grim. "Fiona overdosed on Propranolol—her blood pressure medication. The empty bottle was near her body when we found her. There was a partial print on her prescription bottle that doesn't match Fiona's. I've asked Elliot for his prints to rule them out. He swears he didn't handle her medication. He says she kept it in a cupboard in the kitchen and took it each morning when she made her tea so she wouldn't forget to take it."

Shane frowned. "The finger print alone doesn't mean much, does it? A friend could have been visiting and handled it. She might have asked them to hand her the bottle?"

Garret shook his head. "We found something else. There were traces of Rohypnol on the bottle."

"Rohypnol? The date rape drug?"

"That's the one."

"Was it in her system?"

Garret shook his head. "It's too hard to tell right now. It won't show up in the blood or urine. They have to test her hair to know for sure and those results will take time."

"What the hell, Garret?"

"I know. I can't believe I almost missed this." Garret looked wrecked.

"You wouldn't have. You asked for an autopsy and you hadn't made up your mind one way or the other about her death. You only told the daughter it looked like suicide." He had a feeling nothing he said would ease Garret's conscience.

Garret didn't answer. "You knew her better than I did. Who are the people in her life I should be looking at? I need to look at Elliot. It's a given, but who else?"

Shane rubbed his chest as though he could make the

uneasy ache disappear. "I think Elliot lost his wife years ago. I don't remember the details. He didn't live in town when it happened, but of course the story went around when he moved here. And Fiona has an ex-husband, but they seemed to be on decent terms. They'd argue sometimes, but not much. I mean, they went through the tough part of getting the divorce years ago and there weren't any custody issues because their daughter was an adult at the time."

"Did you represent Fiona in the divorce?"

"No. She had already started the divorce when she moved to town, so she used an out-of-town lawyer."

"You have her ex-husband's name?" Garret took out his phone and opened the notes app.

"Aengus O'Malley. He's got a bit of a temper, but I think he's just loud that way. When Fiona sold her house to Elliot, he came tearing into my office one day telling me he planned to sue me for letting the sale happen."

Garret's brows shot up.

"Yeah, it was ridiculous. He just wanted to blow off steam."

"Elliot owns Fiona's house? I just assumed it was hers."

"Oh, yeah. Most people around town know, I think. It wasn't any secret. Fiona wanted money to travel and things, even though Elliot could have paid for that. She sold him the house so she could contribute to some of what she wanted them to be able to do together."

"Are you sure it was her idea?" Garret asked.

"I think so. And like I told Aengus the day he came into my office, the sale was perfectly legit. She owned the house flat out. I think she bought it with the money the couple divided from the proceeds of the family home in the divorce. She and Elliot had two realtors come in and price the home for her, and the price he paid was based on what the realtors said the comparables were worth."

Garret nodded and made a few more notes. "You know where the husband lives?"

"I think he's over in Johnson City, same as the daughter. They were a lot closer than Fiona and her mom," Shane said.

"Yeah, I got that. The daughter didn't seem like she could get out of town fast enough after the funeral."

Shane sighed. "She blamed Fiona for the divorce. It was Fiona's decision to leave, and Aengus wanted her back. I think he tried to resolve things for a year or more, but Fiona always said she simply wasn't in love with him. Fiona and her daughter seemed to make up for a while there, but when Elliot came along, that strained things again. It was hard for her daughter to accept having a man so much younger than her mom in Fiona's life. They weren't completely estranged or anything. Fiona visited her grandchildren, but I don't think she and her daughter were ever really close again after the divorce."

"Anyone else you can think of who might have had a reason to hurt Fiona?"

Shane rubbed at his jaw. "I can't think of anyone. She and Elliot were the kind to make friends, not enemies. You know Elliot owns the pharmacy in town?" He received a nod from Garret. "He still runs it most days, and Fiona spent her days down at the senior center. Elliot brought in another pharmacist last year to cover a few days a week or when he and Fiona went on trips. They liked to travel."

Shane didn't think you could get Rohypnol in US pharmacies. He was pretty sure that was something you'd have to buy on the street, but he didn't ask.

"Do you know where they traveled to recently?"

Shane thought back to the conversations he'd had with Fiona. "They tried to keep it to places they could fly directly out of Austin, since it was a long drive to the airport and then a flight. She talked about trying to do a trip to Europe, but she hated the idea of spending so much time traveling instead of enjoying the destination. Mostly they went to New Orleans, I think Mexico a few times because she liked the Mayan ruins. I think Memphis once or twice. Bev would know for sure. She and Fiona were very close."

"Did she and Elliot have any big fights or arguments that you know of?"

Shane shook his head. "Nothing I'm aware of." It gave him a sick feeling, but he knew why Garret was asking. Whoever drugged Fiona had to be someone close to her. Someone she would have taken food or a drink from.

"So, you think someone slipped Rohypnol into her food or a drink and then, what, forced the pills down her throat?" Hell, the thought left him cold. Who would have done that?

Garret shook his head. "I don't think they'd have been able to force her to swallow the pills. But with Rohypnol in her system, they might have been able to put the blood pressure medication into her food or drink without her tasting it. The Rohypnol is tasteless. The blood pressure medication would have been harder to cover up, although it's not actually that bad. The medical examiner said there was a famous case of a guy's salad being laced with Propranolol."

"Was there anything else in the autopsy results?" Shane asked.

Garret appeared to be weighing how much to tell Shane, but he must have come out on the side of sharing. "I probably don't need to tell you this all needs to be kept confidential, but I will anyway. It might become crucial to have information no one knows outside of the investigation team during questioning."

"Absolutely. I understand."

"She was drinking alcohol. Whiskey, to be exact."

Shane snorted. "Yeah, she did that. I mean," he rushed to say, "not to excess or anything. She and Bev would try different cocktails out on the porch in the evenings one or two nights a month. They'd call it their around-the-world club. They'd have margaritas one night and then try Saki another. She liked trying different drinks. Said she'd lived her life for other people and drank wine because it was expected of her. This was about 'breaking the mold,' she'd tell me."

He grinned when he said it, remembering the way Fiona liked to break the mold. She liked anything that got her out of any category people expected her to be in. She said she'd spent most of her life in a box and she wouldn't stay there a minute longer.

Garret made a few more notes, then stood and offered his hand to Shane. "Thanks, Shane. I'm sure it'll get around town soon that we have reason to question the suicide, but I appreciate you keeping everything else confidential."

Shane walked Garret to the door and said goodbye, letting his eyes trail across his porch to the small house Elliot and Fiona had shared. The house was dark, save for a single light burning in the living room and Shane had a feeling Elliot was sitting in the near-dark alone, thinking about Fiona.

It startled Shane when the front door opened and Beverly stepped out. He stepped back into the shadow of his porch and watched as she pulled the door shut, then hurried across to her own porch.

Shane stepped into his own house and shut the door. There was nothing wrong with Bev going over to comfort Elliot or to check on him. And yet here Shane was, questioning her motives. It was a shitty feeling when you started questioning all your neighbors' motives and wondering if they'd had a hand in the death of a friend.

28

Coffee: Serenity in a Cup.

— Seen somewhere on a t-shirt and recorded in
Fiona O'Malley's Journal

"This town is cute." Her father looked around the diner. He'd taken them to the last booth and sat facing the door, so he had the view of the entire place.

Phoebe knew what he'd be seeing. Groups of friends or families tucked into booths, the two sisters who owned the diner bickering as one served food and the other cooked and dished it up. There would be tourists, too, discovering Evers for the first time.

"It is," she said, a genuine smile crossing her lips. "I really like it."

"And you're dating your boss." It wasn't a question.

"I don't think I'll discuss that with you, Dad." She said this with just as much finality in her voice as he had in his, but there was affection there to temper the bite of her refusal.

"We'll see," he mumbled into his cup as he tried the coffee. His brows went up at the first sip. "This isn't diner coffee," he said.

"No, it's not, and thank heavens for that." Gina quipped, one hand on her hip as she approached. "I take that back. You can thank me."

"Dad, this is Gina. She and her sister Tina own the diner."

Phoebe almost laughed at the look on her dad's face. He stood. He actually stood and shook Gina's hand. "It's a pleasure to meet you. Tell me, Gina, did you make the coffee?"

Gina fanned herself and Phoebe didn't know whether to laugh or gag. She knew her dad was a good-looking man. She wasn't sure she'd ever seen him flirt, though. He held Gina's hand between his two and waited for her to answer as though his life depended on the question.

"I did, handsome. I sure did," she said with a wink in his direction. "It's my own special blend I mix from five roasts."

Okay, gagging was going to win out. She wasn't sure she'd ever have picked Gina out as a woman who would entice her dad. The woman had blonde hair that came out of a bottle, just as clearly as her sister's bright red did. Despite her heavy figure, Phoebe had always thought she was pretty, with a wide smile for everyone, but she still wouldn't guess Gina was her father's type of pretty. She wasn't sure why, though. Part of it was probably that she hadn't ever seen her dad date or flirt with a woman in front of her.

Had her father hidden his dating from her all these years? She'd always kind of thought he didn't date, but maybe she'd been wrong.

Her father slid back into his seat as Gina took a notepad from her pocket. She nodded and called out a greeting and Phoebe turned to see the man she thought was Aengus O'Malley slide into the booth behind them. Phoebe waved, as well. She didn't know him well, but everyone in town waved when they saw anyone else. It was how the town was. Even if the person was only in town occasionally, like Aengus.

"Be right with you, honey," Gina said, then turned her smile back to Phoebe's father. "All right, big guy, what can I get for you?" She said this *you* in a different way than Phoebe had ever heard. There was an emphasis on it, as though for him, Gina might just run back behind the grill and get his food herself, and they all knew that wasn't going to happen. Well, come to think of it, her father wouldn't know that, but anyone in town knew Gina couldn't cook worth a lick. She handled the coffee and the tables, and Tina took care of the food.

"I'll do the Full Plate Breakfast special with sausage and an extra side of bacon."

"A man who can eat. I like that." Another wink.

Phoebe resisted the urge to roll her eyes.

"And for you, Phoebe?"

"I'll have the French Toast, please."

"Fruit instead of bacon, right?" Gina turned to the General. "It's how she always orders it."

"She's always been healthier than I am." Now her father

was looking at her and smiling the kind of smile that said he was proud of her, and Phoebe found herself forgetting all about the disgusting display of flirting. She missed him. It was nice having him visit her here, even if it was going to be a short visit.

Gina was all smiles as she walked away to hand the order ticket to her sister.

"So, tell me about your work. You like it?" Her dad asked.

Phoebe smiled. "I do."

"So, I was right," Her father sat back, one large arm going up on the booth as he looked at her with his eyes laughing.

"About what?" She was shaking her head already even though she had no idea what he was about to claim credit for.

"Your paralegal degree. I was right that getting it was a good backup."

Phoebe tilted her head in acknowledgement. "All right, I'll give you that one. It turns out, I really do like it."

"It's just you and Shane there?"

"Ah, now I see where you're going with this. I told you, I'm not going to discuss that with you. But, no, it's not just us. Margaret is the receptionist and all-around office manager. I can't believe he was holding down the place without a paralegal for so long. People come to him for everything. Not just for work, either. People come in and out throughout the day to ask his take on things. It's kind of nice to see the way the town trusts him."

Her father murmured a response, but it sounded like he wasn't quite ready to buy into the Shane Bishop fan club.

"I mean it. His neighbor, for example, she died recently. She asked Shane before she died to take care of some things she'd left in a safe deposit box."

"What kind of things?"

Phoebe shrugged. "It wasn't anything of great value, but the point was, she trusted him to get them to the people she cared about. Letters for her boyfriend and a journal she wanted her daughter to read." Phoebe's face fell. "Her daughter didn't read it. It's sad. She's really angry. Her mom and she hadn't been getting along. Shane asked me to read the journal to see if I could figure out any way to help us get through to the daughter. It's that kind of thing. It's more than just a job here. It's the community. It's like being a part of a larger family."

Phoebe bit down on her lip, afraid she might have hurt her dad's feelings. It had always just been she and her grandmother and him. Now, she and her dad were all that was left.

He didn't seem to notice. "So, have you found anything that might help? Anything in the journal that might tell you how to help the daughter come to terms with whatever was going on between her and her mother?"

"No. I haven't gotten into it as much as I'd like, but I will. She was a fascinating woman. I was sorry I never had the chance to meet her. She seemed to be so full of life, like she never hesitated to just grab life and live it." Phoebe thought again how shocking it had been to read the journal knowing Fiona had taken her own life. It struck her every time she read the entries, but the entries she was reading were from years before. She guessed a lot could change in the inter-vening years.

After her father left for his flight Sunday evening, Phoebe pulled out Fiona's journal. So far, she hadn't found anything in it that she thought might instantly make Fiona's daughter forgive Fiona. It was more the entirety of the journey her mother took within the pages that Emmaline would need to see. Fiona had talked some about her child-hood in Ireland and about the feeling of excitement when she and Aengus had come to America together. A lot of what Fiona felt for Aengus seemed to be tied up in the idea of him taking her away from her family to explore new and exciting things.

She'd been so young when she and Aengus met. Having seen Aengus O'Malley, Phoebe could imagine how he'd seemed larger than life to a young woman. Young girl, really.

It turned out, there just wasn't enough there between Fiona and Aengus to sustain a lifetime together.

Phoebe wondered if what she felt for Shane was enough to last a lifetime. Part of her said it could be, but another part was also scared. She was also realistic enough to know she hadn't known him long enough to make that decision.

She was surprised by that. She'd often been ruled by her emotions and hadn't really been one to slow herself down long enough to think things through. She liked that she was growing enough as a person to do that.

Still, the kick in her chest every time she thought about Shane told her this could go somewhere, if she let it.

She settled into the journal, willing thoughts of Shane

from her mind. As much as she loved the start of a relationship where all you could think about was the other person, it did feel a tad obsessive.

June 21, 2014 Emmaline called today and for once, we talked like old times. I think she might be on the brink of finally, truly forgiving me for leaving Aengus. She'll never see my side of it, but that's more than I can hope for, I think.

Today, she told me she's dating someone she's really excited about. His name is Robert, and she met him through a work colleague. She sounds excited, and I'm glad for her. I didn't have the heart to tell her about Elliot yet. Oh, I haven't told you, Dear Diary, about Elliot, have I? I suppose I've been busy being swept off my feet.

I felt a little foolish when he first asked me out, but then I remembered my commitment to living my life to the fullest, and I said screw it. Oh, how Aengus would cringe if he heard how crass I've become.

Oh well, screw it! Ha! Look at me go.

Elliot moved to town to buy the pharmacy from the old geezer who used to own it. Grumpy old son of a gun, I tell you. Well, it's a right nice twist to have a friendlier face in there. At first, I assumed he flirted with everyone, but Bev told me he doesn't treat her the way he treats me. She said he's friendly enough, but, as she put it, there are no goo goo eyes for her when he's doling out her arthritis medication. She sounded a little put out at first, but she seems to be over that.

Of course, the whole town will have a field day when they find out we're dating. We've kept it secret for a week, but I don't think that's going to last much longer.

The fact that Elliot's new in town alone was enough to start the rumor mill going. Everyone always wants to know every scrip, scrap, and strudel from a body's past when someone comes to town. Elliot's story is tragic, really. Horrible thing for him to have gone through. His wife died, poor dear, and she was five months pregnant. There was no saving the baby. Elliot came home to find his wife had collapsed. It was some kind of allergic reaction. She was prescribed medicine she didn't know she was allergic to. They couldn't save her or the baby. I can't imagine his pain. It seems it would leave a hole that would never be filled no matter that you find the strength to move on.

Of course, that was ten years ago. Even so, the town is having a field day with it. I'm not going to worry about the rumor mill for now, though. He makes me happy. And Emmaline sounds happy. For now, that's more than enough for me!

Phoebe closed the journal and sighed. It was horrible, reading about Elliot's wife, but the way Fiona had decided to grab life and live it no matter what others thought made Phoebe want to be that bold.

She had a feeling Chelsea had been right about some of what she had said. Phoebe had been afraid to commit to someone, to a life with another person. And she knew why. She was too afraid she'd end up being like her own mother. That she wouldn't be able to hack it and she'd leave.

That fear, though, had ended up leaving her side-lined in a way. Most people might look at Phoebe and say she'd been grabbing life and living it. In some ways, she had. She'd tried a lot of things she wanted to try. She'd jumped around to jobs that had interested her. The only reason she had a paralegal degree was because her father had talked her into getting it years ago as a backup plan to her fly-by-the-seat-of-her-pants attitude.

But, she knew the truth was she'd been living her life that way because it meant not having to create ties. Not having to grab what she *really* wanted. Not having to test if she was capable of commitment, of love, of building a life and a family with one person. Or if she, like her mother, was somehow deficient.

Phoebe went to her closet and pulled out the small box of letters she'd written to her mom over the years. She ran her hand over the cover of the box, not at all sure she was ready to open this particular area of her life again. These letters had been written over the course of years, and they spelled out the pain she'd felt for her mother's betrayal in harsh relief. With a deep breath, she cracked the lid, and she would swear a wave of heartache swept out like a dark cloud. It was always that way. Her mother's memory was just that. A dark cloud that dimmed whatever light Phoebe had let into her life.

29

However long the day, night must fall.

— Irish proverb recorded in Fiona O'Malley's
Journal

P hoebe was the first to arrive at the office the following morning. She was caught up on her work and probably didn't need to keep coming in so early, but she'd found she liked the quiet of the morning. It wasn't exactly quiet since she tended to blast music while she worked, but it was her time alone in the office. The rest of the office lay dormant and she didn't need to worry she might bother Shane or Margaret.

She was here earlier than usual today. Sleep hadn't come very easily to her the night before. She'd been tossing and turning with thoughts of Fiona and Elliot and her own worry about whether she had it in her to be the kind of person who could stay with a family or not.

She'd ended up sitting on the floor of her room looking over the letters she'd written but not sent to her mother over the years. She'd only sent the one. When she hadn't gotten a reply, she'd stopped sending them, but she hadn't stopped writing to her.

But it turned out, there were no answers for her in the letters shoved in a box in her closet. At five in the morning, she'd given up. She'd showered and dressed, then looked at the letters one last time before shoving them back into the closet.

She needed to let go of her mother. It was time to say goodbye to the ghost of a woman who wasn't dead, but might as well be for all the care she'd ever had for her only daughter.

A half hour later, she let herself into the lobby of the law firm and flicked the lights on. A loud crash came from the back of the office.

"Shane? Is that you?" She started toward the noise, then froze. A shiver skated across the back of Phoebe's neck as she realized Shane would have turned the lights on in the back hallway if he'd come in that way. And if he'd walked to work as she had and entered through the front door, he would have turned on the lobby lights.

"Shane." She whispered the word this time holding her breath for a minute.

She couldn't ignore the hairs on the back of her neck that told her to leave. If for no other reason, her dad would kill her if something happened and he found out she hadn't listened to her instincts. Instincts were everything, he'd always told her.

She turned and went back out the way she'd come.

On the sidewalk, her chest felt tight and she fumbled with her cell phone as she looked around. The street was empty and too still. What had felt peaceful moments before now felt isolated. At this time, the diner around the corner and the feed store might have customers, but this side of town housed the law firm and several artist's galleries. None of those businesses were open yet.

Screw the phone. Phoebe looked over her shoulder as she hustled around the corner to the police station. She flew through the doors, letting out a breath to find one of Garret's patrol officers standing at a desk looking up at her in surprise.

"Ms. Joy? Are you all right?"

Phoebe looked down to see her hands were shaking, but she suddenly felt foolish. She'd likely just completely over-reacted. She'd probably burst into the police station all because some of the extra pens and copy paper Margaret kept on the shelves by the back door had worked their way off a shelf.

"Hey, Phoebe, what's going on?" Garret entered the room from his office off the main area.

"I...I'm sorry, I..."

"Okay," Garret said moving forward and taking her by the arms to move her into a chair. "Take a breath, Phoebe."

She did, and it came out as a laugh. She rubbed her hands over her face. "I'm sorry. This is silly. I just went to the office early and it was dark when I got there. I heard a noise in the back and I freaked." She looked up at him. "Oh, God and I just ran out of there and left the front door unlocked."

He smiled. "No worries. I'll just walk down with you and we'll be sure things are okay. I'd rather have a false alarm where everyone's safe than you ending up like the stupid person in a horror movie who goes to investigate the noise. We all know how that turns out."

Phoebe laughed and stood up, wrapping her hands around her waist. "Thank you, Garret. I'll still feel like an idiot when it turns out to be nothing."

30

A man may live after losing his life, but not after losing his honor.

— Irish proverb recorded in Fiona O'Malley's
Journal

I t didn't turn out to be nothing. Phoebe stood in her
office looking at the disarray. It hadn't been trashed,
exactly, but whoever had gone through her drawers hadn't
bothered being neat about it. There were open drawers,
their contents strewn on the floor.

"Shane's on his way," Garret said, stepping back into the
room. He had cleared the building when they arrived and
found it empty, but it was clear someone had been there. A
window in the back hall had been broken as the point-of-
entry. "Does it look like there's anything missing to you?"

"I don't know." Phoebe walked around the room looking
at the contents of her office laid out on the floor. He'd

already told her not to touch anything. "I don't think so. It's hard to remember everything that was here, but nothing strikes me as missing."

He held up a case she hadn't even known he was carrying. It looked like a dark blue tackle box for fishing. "I'm going to see if I can lift any prints from the window sill and then I'll come in and check the drawers. Are you all right here?"

Phoebe nodded. "I'll sit out here," she said, moving toward the chairs in the lobby. The lobby hadn't been touched.

The front door flew open and Shane came in, white as a sheet. His eyes found her and she stood.

There was no time for explanations or answers.

She was in Shane's arms, wrapped in warmth and comfort and safety. Strong muscles held her and she rested her head against his chest. It was silly how much her heart was still pounding, and how much having him there to hold her helped. It wasn't like she'd been here when the burglar broke in. It wasn't like she'd seen him or interrupted him or had to fight anyone off.

Then something else occurred to Phoebe. Her heart wasn't the only one pounding. Shane's heart slammed in his chest, racing, as though he'd just gone ten rounds with someone.

Phoebe slid her hand to his heart and pulled back to look him in the eye. "Are you okay?"

"I'm supposed to ask you that." His voice was low and he looked over her as though he needed to see for himself that the answer was yes.

"I'm fine. I heard something at the back of the office as soon as I turned on the lights. Garret thinks they were either on their way out or they ran as soon as I turned the lights on."

Shane let out a breath and leaned against her, nuzzling into her. He just stayed there, holding her and she stayed in his arms, not making any attempt to pull away.

She didn't want to, she realized. She never wanted to pull away. She liked the way he made her feel. Liked the way she felt safe, treasured, wanted. Like she mattered.

31

You have only to let joy into your heart to find it in your life.

— FIONA O'MALLEY'S JOURNAL

Shane tried to listen to what Garret was saying, but his focus was on Phoebe. He'd been such an idiot. He'd thought about putting in an alarm over the years, but he hadn't ever gotten around to it. This was Evers. If there was a break-in around here, it was teens messing around, and they never bothered with his office. He didn't have anything exciting enough to entice them.

"Can you think of any reason anyone would want to break in?"

"No," Shane said in response to Garret. He was pretty sure Garret had repeated the question for a second time for him after he'd missed it the first time. His eyes kept going back to where Phoebe sat with Margaret in the lobby. The color was back in Phoebe's cheeks and she was laughing at something Margaret said.

"Did you have a chance to look through your office and see what might be missing?" Garret asked the question with the kind of look that told Shane he knew exactly where Shane's mind was and that it sure as hell wasn't in the conversation they were having.

Shane refocused on his friend. "Yeah. There's nothing missing that I can see. We keep our client files in locked cabinets overnight and the archived files are in a locked closet or at a separate storage facility once they hit the one-year mark. If someone was looking for a client file or information on our clients, they didn't get it." He'd checked and the closet and filing cabinets had been locked and hadn't been tampered with.

"And they —"

Shane cut in. "Didn't get in them."

"Has anyone threatened you lately or been harassing you about anything? Even something small?"

The two men turned as Sheriff John Davies entered the building. He removed his hat and nodded to Phoebe and Margaret before approaching the two men.

"Shane, Garret," he said with a nod. "Your dispatcher told me what happened when I stopped into the station. Thought I'd swing by and see if there's anything I can help with."

John Davies had been the Sheriff in the county for several years. Before the town established its own police force the year before, he'd been in charge of all law enforcement in the area. More importantly, he was friends with both Shane and Cade, and was on good terms with Garret. Shane had no doubt his offer came from a genuine desire to help, not some competitive need to butt into an investigation where his help wasn't needed.

Garret seemed to take it that way, as well. He grinned, for once letting the seriousness of the situation drop. "If you could help my uncooperative witness focus on the investigation instead of his paralegal, that might move things along."

Shane crossed his arms over his chest and glared at the two men standing before him. "Funny."

It wasn't, though. His heart was still pounding, and it showed no signs of stopping. When he'd heard Phoebe had interrupted a break-in, the panic had been immediate, nearly taking him out at the knees.

Garret and John shared a grin before Garret repeated his question. "You were about to tell me if anyone has been harassing you or might have threatened you lately. Is anyone angry at you over any cases? Anything in your personal life?"

Shane sighed and rubbed the back of his neck. "Tim Devos isn't thrilled with me. He took a swing at me recently."

"When was this?" Garret asked.

Shane thought back. "Couple of weeks?"

John didn't look surprised. "He's been unraveling since Maryann left him."

"I know, but it still honestly took me by surprise. I thought he was a good guy. I think he might be drinking, though. He's been calling her, showing up at all hours. Sometimes he's begging her to take him back. Other times, he's agitated and angry. He's threatened her. I had to get a restraining order for her. He didn't like it, so he let me know that."

"With his fist?" Garret asked.

Shane shrugged. "Tried. Didn't land it. I talked to his lawyer. She said she'd try to talk some sense into her client and that was it. I haven't heard from him since then and as far as I know, neither has Maryann."

"Anyone else you can think of?" Garret asked.

"Sometimes even a small disagreement can make someone lash out like this," John added. Garret nodded his agreement.

"Nothing that I can think of."

Garret gave him the *if you think of anything else* spiel. He'd already told Shane there hadn't been any prints on the windowsill or the drawer pulls in either office, but based on the smudge marks, he thought the person had worn gloves.

To Shane, that didn't sound like the act of a ticked off soon-to-be ex-husband. It sounded a lot more calculated and planned than Shane would have liked.

32
___

You can't find love if you aren't willing to risk your heart. Sadly,
love simply isn't safe and neat that way.

— Fiona O'Malley's Journal

Phoebe wondered if it would be wrong to admit to Shane that she'd been feeling nervous and overly vulnerable all day. Then again, he'd been in uber-protective mode and had checked on her every hour, at least. Now, as they walked home from dinner, she felt edgy. She wanted to ask him to come up and stay with her for a while, but wasn't sure how to ask. She didn't want to sound like she was blatantly inviting him in for sex.

Of course, with the way he'd stroked her wrist during dinner, she'd be lying if she said she wasn't a little interested in sex. He'd held one hand on top of hers while they talked at the end of their meal, letting his thumb trace small circles over her wrist in a move that was a lot more erotic than she though it would be. How a simple touch of his thumb on her skin could set her off so much was beyond her. She wondered if he knew what it was doing to her.

They stopped at the bottom of her stairs and he pulled her into his arms. She was quickly realizing she loved this man's arms. They felt so amazing. She'd dated plenty of strong men but somehow, his arms always seemed to feel stronger to her. Like he could hold the world and not let things spin out of control.

But then he dipped his head and kissed her and things spun very much out of control. In a good way.

Her whole body reacted to the touch of his mouth on hers. He ran a hand up her back, cradling her head and tilting her as though he wanted her just so. Just so, so that he could deepen the kiss and drive her mad.

And she had zero problem with that control.

Phoebe moaned, and she heard a deep growl come from his chest in response.

He moved to her neck and Phoebe took advantage, whispering in his ear. She suddenly didn't care one bit if it seemed like she was inviting him up for sex. She was.

She didn't care about anything other than feeling his hands all over her right now. And that wasn't going to happen if they stood at the bottom of the stairs much longer.

"Take me upstairs, Shane."

She'd scarcely spoken when he lifted her feet a few inches off the ground, still connected at the mouth, arms locked tightly around her. She would have laughed if he hadn't stolen her breath with the move. He took them up, one step at a time, cranking her arousal higher still as he teased and taunted with kisses, licks, nibbles.

At the top of the stairs, he set her down and spun her toward the door so she could unlock it. When she did, he lifted her off the ground again, this time scooping her up in his arms with a grin.

Phoebe laughed this time, and wrapped her arms around his neck. He was being playful, and it was somehow almost as sexy as his moves on the stairs had been.

He shut the door with his foot and headed to the right, toward her bedroom. The apartment was nothing more than a large box, but it had windows all around, making it bright in the daytime. The living room was in the front, with her bedroom off to the right at the front of the space. At the back, the living room blended into a kitchen with windows lining the whole room and a back door that led to a narrow staircase out into the yard.

She didn't much care about any of that now. She cared about the bedroom, and he seemed to be in sync on that. He set her down in front of her bed and framed her face with his hands. "I had planned to wait, Phoebe. I thought we would wait until we were sure this was headed someplace, but then you went and wore that dress."

His gaze swept over her coral red dress and it might as well have been his hands for the effect it had on her. She heated and her belly thrummed with anticipation.

As though he'd guessed at the effect of those words, he ran his fingertips lightly down her arms, but let his words continue to do the work. "Through the entire meal, I watched these straps—" he ran a finger under each of the spaghetti straps—"I watched them and wanted to know what it would feel like to run my tongue along the soft skin beneath them. To feel you shiver when I moved to your neck."

She shivered in response. She couldn't help it. It was as if her body had ceded control to his words.

"Or maybe you'd rather I moved down." He ran his fingers down to her breasts, letting them glide lightly over the cups of her breasts.

She let out a small moan and his eyes flared with heat.

"I wondered if you'd be angry with me for tearing your dress. I wasn't sure I had the patience to take it off carefully." He slid his hands up and slipped the spaghetti straps from her shoulders. "But now, seeing the way your body responds to slow teasing—" he shook his head —"I find I have the patience after all."

"Please," Phoebe whispered, and he only gave a wolfish grin in response. He loosened the two buttons at her breasts and let the fabric slide down to expose her skin.

Shane knelt then, worshipping the globes he'd exposed. First with soft touches of his hands, then with his breath, blowing gently on her skin. She would swear she had burst into flames. The heat of his mouth was on her, exploring the swell of her breasts and she stopped breathing.

"God, Shane, please." She whimpered it as prayer and plea. He moved to her nipple, still covered by the lacy demi bra she'd worn for their date. His tongue swirled over her and she cried out.

His hands came up, cupping her bottom and he squeezed gently. "You're killing me, Phoebe." He whispered, and she wanted to object. To tell him he was the one doing the slaying, but she couldn't find the words. They caught with the breath in her throat as he moved to the next nipple.

By the time he moved them to the bed and lay by her side, she was a quivering pile of mush. He ran a hand up her thigh, spreading her legs and slipping his fingers into her panties. She knew she was wet and swollen and so damned ready for him, it was almost embarrassing. But she couldn't feel any embarrassment. She could only feel *him*. Feel what he was doing to her. How he'd teased her into a frenzy.

Shane slid down her body and tugged her panties to the side, licking and teasing until she thought she might lose her mind. She fisted the comforter and bucked beneath him. She lost count of how many times she'd said please, and then his fingers entered her. When he sucked on her clitoris, she came in a hard-rushing wave.

She emerged from the haze he'd left her in to find he'd stripped himself bare and was sheathing himself in a condom. She had the errant thought somewhere in the back of her mind that they should be taking this more slowly. It didn't last. As she watched him, she lost all will to put this off. She wanted him, wanted to be with him. In so many ways.

It wasn't only physical, although obviously at this moment, the physical part of things was ruling her thoughts. But with Shane, her feelings seemed to go so much deeper. When he moved over her on the bed, capturing her mouth again as he entered her, she would swear the connection went so much deeper. Much deeper than any she'd had before. And she lost herself to it.

Emotion and sensation and, maybe, magic, seemed to combine to sweep her away. Phoebe cried out as a second orgasm mounted and Shane groaned her name in her ear. She could feel his orgasm gathering. She ran her nails down his back and he tensed, saying her name again as the orgasm took hold. The sound of her name on his tongue capped the moment as they rode through the orgasm together, pleasure and happiness coursing through her.

When it was over, she snuggled into him, and he pulled her into his arms and turned onto his side next to her.

It wasn't until hours later that she awoke to find Shane getting dressed in the early morning light.

He looked over at her, a slow smile spreading on his face. "I didn't want to wake you," he said, as he leaned in to kiss her.

"You're leaving? What time is it?"

"It's almost six. I have to run home and shower and shave. I've got court this afternoon, so I need a suit."

She nodded and he smiled down at her. "Get some more sleep."

She shook her head. "I'll walk you out."

He pulled her into a one-armed grip when she stepped from bed. "You'll tempt me right back in there."

Phoebe laughed. "I was thinking of showering and getting an early start."

He groaned. "You're killing me, Phoebe. Killing me."

33

May the saddest day of your future be no worse than the happiest day of your past.

— IRISH PROVERB RECORDED IN FIONA O'MALLEY'S
JOURNAL

Two hours later, Phoebe looked up to find Laura headed toward her on the sidewalk outside the office. Phoebe hadn't fallen back to sleep after Shane left, so it seemed a waste to sit at home.

"What are you doing out and about so early?" She asked as Laura approached and hugged her.

"Meeting Cade for breakfast. He had to drive a few towns over to drop off a dog he was working with so we're going to meet for breakfast at the diner."

Phoebe smiled.

"Listen," Laura said, "I was so shocked the other day, I

don't think I thanked you properly for helping Shane track down the information on my brother."

"Oh, you're welcome. I was happy to do it. My dad said he'll talk to more people when he gets back. I think he's taking it really personally that James might have been left behind without the Army going in to get him out."

The new security system began the countdown beep letting Phoebe know she had thirty seconds to enter her code. She punched in the digits with a glance at Laura. Shane had paid extra for a company to install the system the day before. She didn't want to know how much he'd had to pay for that, but she did have to admit, it made her feel better.

"I heard about the break-in. It's a good thing you weren't here any earlier. You might have gotten hurt."

Phoebe nodded. She had to admit, she was still a little freaked out about that. She had thought she was being stupid, walking out and going to the police station, but now she was glad she had.

When she talked to her dad by phone, he'd been glad she had, too. "That's my girl," he had said. She only laughed in response. He had drilled safety into her as a child and that was one of the lessons. You leave, you go get help.

Phoebe smiled at Laura now as they walked into her office. "Shane made me promise not to come to the office before eight unless he's meeting me here. Actually, he was pushing for nine since he never comes in later than that, but I talked him down to eight."

"I bet he was freaked out."

Phoebe's smile was rueful. "A little." Searching for a

subject change, she went with the next obvious choice. "So, did you go see your mother-in-law? I mean your former mother-in-law?"

Laura nodded. "Honestly, I was surprised by her reaction. I know she's changed a lot, but when I told her what you discovered, her immediate response was that we needed to get him out of there. She had picked up the phone before I could say another word. She's calling in as many favors as she can."

"I hope it helps." Phoebe sank into her chair. She didn't have a brother, but if her dad was missing and she didn't know if he was dead or alive, the pain would kill her. She looked up at Laura. "I'm sorry. I don't even know if it's easier or harder now that you know he might be...."

Laura seemed to understand what she was saying. She smiled a little, but it was the kind of smile that held sorrow. "It's harder in some ways, but if there's even a chance he's alive..." She shook her head as though she couldn't find words for what that would mean to her, and Phoebe imagined she couldn't.

Phoebe stood and wrapped her arms around Laura and hugged her again.

"Thank you," Laura whispered. "Thank you for giving me the possibility of finding him."

When Laura had left, Phoebe thought about going in to see Shane but then thought she might surprise him with coffee and pastries from the diner. She could be down and back in a few minutes, and she really needed the coffee. They could sit and have a breakfast of sorts together before Margaret got into the office.

She smiled to herself as she walked the short distance to the diner.

"Well, don't you look pretty today."

Phoebe turned to see June Leary—or maybe it was June Jubie—smiling at her.

"Hi June," she said. "And thank you. I feel pretty today." Phoebe almost laughed to herself.

"I should introduce you to a friend of mine. You'd love him, and I think he's just your type. He's an artist. He does the most incredible sculptures." She winked at Phoebe. "Good hands, you know. That's the key to a good man. Of course, Jake and I would never date. We're too much like brother and sister, but you would just adore him, I think."

"Oh." Phoebe didn't know what else to say to that. She and June moved to the side as a group of tourists made their way through the diner door. "Thanks, I um…"

"Oh! I'm sorry. Are you still seeing Shane? I just assumed that was over already. Shane doesn't like commitment. He's one of *those* men." She looked at Phoebe with a conspiratorial grin. "I mean, don't get me wrong. He's fun and as far as I'm concerned, you should ride this one out as long as he'll have you."

She laughed as though she had made the funniest joke in the world and Phoebe choked out a laugh with her, all the while feeling like her face might crack. Much the way her heart was cracking.

June didn't seem to notice. In fact, for a minute, she seemed lost in sadness herself, as if she were the one of them putting on a brave face. "I've decided, that's the way to handle a man like Shane Bishop. Walk away before he can walk away from you!"

Phoebe wasn't sure she was breathing.

The other June—whichever one she was—and Mindy walked up, all smiles.

"What are you two laughing about?" Mindy said with a quirk of her head.

Phoebe opened her mouth, wanting to say nothing and nip the conversation in the bud.

June—the first one—had other ideas. "We're commiserating about Shane Bishop and his unmarriageable ways."

"Oh, honey." June the second shook her head, but then gave Phoebe a wistful grin. "Enjoy it while it lasts. It's a hell of a ride."

Phoebe blinked at the similarity of the comments from the two Junes. She'd been an idiot.

And, God, Chelsea had been right—she just didn't know how right. She'd thought Phoebe was choosing a guy who was unreachable because he was her boss. It turned out, Phoebe was as spot-on at choosing non-committal men as she always had been. She'd just fooled herself again.

"Hey," Mindy said, giving her two friends a sullen look. "Some of us aren't ready to joke about this. I really thought..." She didn't finish but one of the Junes put her arm around Mindy's shoulders and squeezed.

"I'm sorry. You're right. We all thought we were the one to get him to change his ways and tie the knot. Lord knows, that man puts on a good show, doesn't he? I mean, who would think the town lawyer wouldn't be good and ready to settle down?"

"We've had longer to deal with the reality than Mindy," June number two explained to Phoebe with a sympathetic look at Mindy. "She only just threw in the towel a month ago."

"All right, girls," June number one said with a wave of her hand. "Enough about Shotgun Shane. Will you have breakfast with us Phoebe? We were headed into the diner?"

"Oh...uh. Wait, Shotgun Shane?" She looked at the women.

It was June number one who answered with a grin. "Only way to get him to the altar. Shotgun." She winked at Phoebe. "Seriously, let me know when you're finished having fun. I'll set you up with Jake. Don't you think she'd be perfect for Jake?" She said to the others as they all made their way into the diner.

Phoebe didn't listen to the replies. She waved them off and bought herself coffee to go, skipping the cup she'd planned to bring Shane as well as the pastries. She was pretty sure she had a lump of concrete setting in her stomach. There likely wasn't room for anything else in there at the moment.

34

Doesn't it seem like life just shits on you sometimes?

— FIONA O'MALLEY'S JOURNAL

Shane frowned as he realized it was nine o'clock. It might be stupid, but he'd been hoping Phoebe would come see him as soon as she got in. Much as he hated to sound like a lovesick teenager, he'd been hoping she'd been wanting to see him as much as he wanted to see her.

He shoved back from his desk. He wasn't too much of an idiot to go to her instead of waiting for her to come to him. As he rounded his desk, the phone rang.

"Shane Bishop," he said, answering it while standing, with every intention of getting off as fast as he could so he could go see Phoebe.

"Shane, it's Garret. I've got Elliot down at the station to answer some questions about Fiona's death. He's asked for you."

Shane cursed under his breath. "I'll be right there," is what he said into the phone before grabbing his things and heading out of the office. The police station was only around the corner, so he didn't bother with his car.

Minutes later, he found a bleary-eyed Elliot waiting in the small interview room at the police station.

Garret opened the door and let him in. "I'll let you guys have a few minutes to talk before we get started."

Shane nodded and stepped into the room.

"Sorry, Shane. I didn't know who else to ask for, and Bev insisted I shouldn't be alone." Elliot's head hung in the way of a man who'd been defeated by life. Who'd been handed more than his fair share to weather and had decided to throw in the towel instead of fight back.

Shane sat next to him, pulling a notepad and pen from the briefcase he carried. "Did they ask you anything yet?"

Elliot shook his head. "Garret said they found out about my wife. That they needed to bring me in to answer some questions. Bev was there. She said to call you." He repeated the information like a child might.

"Do you know what Garret means? When he says they know about your wife?" Shane knew there had been a tragedy but for the life of him, he couldn't remember what it was.

Now Elliot sighed and rubbed his head, then his eyes, like he could work away the memory. "My wife. It was years ago, Shane. Before I came here. She took some medicine she was allergic to. She didn't know she had an allergy and I wasn't home. She tried to call for help. It was anaphylaxis. It hit so fast and because she didn't know about the allergy, we didn't have an EpiPen or anything like that in the house."

Shane made some notes. "And did Garret say anything about this? Did he say anything to you on the way to the station?"

"No." Elliot looked up again. "There were whispers when Sheila died. I was a pharmacist, people said. How could I not know she could have died from the medicine she took, they said."

"Was there an investigation?"

Elliot shook his head. "I don't think so. It was ruled accidental death." His voice cracked. "But now Fiona. Shane, I didn't hurt Fiona. I didn't hurt my wife or my son. And I didn't hurt Fiona."

Shane was staring at a broken man. He put his hand on Elliot's shoulder and squeezed. "All right. Let's bring Garret in here and get this over with. I want you to pause after each question to give me a chance to object if I'm going to. Don't offer any information. Just answer the question he asks, but nothing more. Do you understand?"

Elliot nodded and Shane went to the door to tap on the glass.

Garret entered minutes later. Garret was a fair man and a good cop. He wouldn't have any interest in arresting the wrong person here. Still, Shane knew he had a job to do and if he thought there was enough reason to question Elliot formally, he would do it without concern for how much Elliot was hurting.

He would do his job and so would Shane.

35

Somedays, I wish I'd stayed in bed.

— FIONA O'MALLEY'S JOURNAL

P hoebe came out of her office as soon as Shane entered. She and Margaret met him with matching expressions of concern.

"You heard?" He directed this toward Phoebe. As much as he'd like to tell himself it was only concern for Elliot he was seeing in her face, he knew something else was off about her.

Nonetheless, she nodded. "Margaret filled me in. How did it go? They're not holding Elliot, are they?"

"Not right now. So far, they don't have much to point to him." His jaw clenched. "Elliot's wife had died years before, but there'd been nothing to indicate foul play other than the whisperings of cruel neighbors. Anyone who'd seen Elliot today would know he was still torn up about his wife and child dying."

There was also the fact Fiona and Elliot had travelled to Mexico several times. Rohypnol could be bought in Mexico. Of course, it could also be bought on the streets in the United States, so those two things alone were weak circumstantial evidence, at best.

Still, Elliot had been shaken by the interrogation. Shane didn't like the way the man's mental health was looking.

Phoebe nodded. "I've got some things I'm in the middle of," she said and vanished back into her office without meeting his eyes.

"Do you need me to do anything for Elliot, Shane?" Margaret asked. If she felt the tension he could feel between him and Phoebe, she didn't mention it. Then again, maybe he was imagining it.

"No. He's home for now. It's a waiting game at this point."

"You've had several messages." She pulled out her notepad and started running through the messages. It was all Shane could do not to toss the notepad across the room and chase after Phoebe.

He waited, though. Got through the message review, went to his office to set his briefcase down, then picked up a folder and casually crossed back through the lobby to Phoebe's office.

She answered his tap with a small, "come in," and he did. As soon as he saw her, he knew he'd been right.

She stood, looking for all the world like she wanted to

take off rather than face him. He tossed the folder on her desk for her to look at later. It wasn't important.

"Tell me what's going on, Phoebe." He was careful, moderating his tone so it wasn't an accusation. Clamping his hands into fists so he didn't go to her and pull her to him, using his mouth to convince her not to do what he knew was about to come.

All morning, he'd been waiting to see her. He'd wanted to see in her eyes that what they'd shared together the night before meant as much as he thought it had. Right now, her expression said anything but.

She tilted her gaze to meet his, but glanced away again just as quickly. "I don't think this is a good idea. I think we made a mistake."

"A mistake?" He repeated the words, hearing them, but still not believing them. She couldn't really believe that. Shane almost wanted to laugh. He'd waited years to find a woman who made him feel as powerfully as Phoebe did, and she was saying he couldn't have her.

"I...it's not...it's just..."

Shane took a breath, then rounded the desk in a few short strides and put his hands on her arms. He forced himself to be patient to rub gently up and down those arms. What he really wanted to do was beg, plead, drop to his knees. "Tell me, Phoebe. Tell me, what has you running? What has you worried? I thought we were having a good time."

He'd said the wrong thing. He'd thought he was being smart, not pressuring her. Not telling her he really thought this could go somewhere between them. He thought maybe if he backed off and let her take things slowly, let her see this was right, she'd be fine.

He was wrong. He could see it the moment he said it.

She'd put up a wall as soon as the words came out of his mouth, and there was no undoing it.

"I don't think this is a good idea. I don't want to be more than your employee."

The word employee felt like ice slipping beneath his skin and crackling down his spine. Because that's what she was. His employee. He couldn't sit here and try to convince her. Convince was too damned close to coerce. He'd been a jackass to try this.

No, much worse than a jackass. He'd been a complete idiot. He was her boss. He shouldn't have ever touched her, no matter what he felt for her or where he thought it might go.

Shane stiffened and stepped back, with a nod. "You got it."

He didn't say anything more before he walked out. Probably couldn't have if he tried. Because he'd really been starting to think—hell, he couldn't even think it to himself. It hadn't been anything. It wasn't going anywhere.

It just wasn't what he thought it was. She'd made that much loud and clear.

Phoebe pressed her hand to her mouth after she watched

Shane leave. She leaned over in her chair as she tried to keep her crying as quiet as possible. She couldn't let Shane or Margaret hear her. The idea of it was mortifying.

She had a feeling she was failing, at least where Margaret was concerned. She turned her music on, leaving it low enough that it wouldn't bother Margaret, but hoped it might muffle the sound as she worked to get herself under control.

She did it. She stopped the tears, but she ended up with one of those painful lumps lodged in her throat. There was no willing that thing away. She had done it to herself. She never should have let this get started. That had been one of the most foolish things she'd done in a long time, and she had a long list of things to choose from.

She breathed long and deep, slowly in through her nose and out through her mouth. She could do this. She *would* do this. She would get through the momentary pain of falling for the wrong man again. Because, that's what this would be, right?

It would hurt and she'd be raw, but she would get through it. And in the end, it would be better this way. She still had a job she loved and a new town and friends she loved. A home.

She blew right past the sense that this was somehow different. That this pain wasn't likely to be washed away with a marathon session of Heath Ledger movies and a few good pints of Rocky Road. She had to, because if she didn't... well, there just wasn't any going there. She *would* forget about Shane and go on with her plan to find a man who didn't break out into hives at the idea of her in a dress saying I Do.

She watched the clock tick down the rest of the day, and could easily say it was the longest day of her life. She wanted nothing more than to go home and hide.

Love isn't going to come easily, and it isn't going to stay easily. You're going to have to fight for it. Then, you'll have to fight and fight some more. It's a fight you'll come to love and a fight you'll come to realize is worth it. Always.

— FIONA O'MALLEY'S JOURNAL

Shane didn't want to see anyone. Laura and Cade would already be up at their house they'd built on the west side of the property, and May and Josh would have long ago gone to bed. Shane was here to visit a ghost.

He pulled his car down the small dirt road that wound around the back side of the rescue barn over to the tinker barn by way of the field, instead of going past the main house. No other ranch in the area had two barns that had ceased to be used for their original purposes in such a drastic fashion.

The rescue barn held animals, but not many of the kind it was intended to. Cade still used one or two of the horse stalls for his horse and whatever horses and donkeys he was rehabbing at the moment. Of course, the stalls were just as likely to hold cats, dogs, pigs, or whatever else found their way to Cade Bishop for rescue and training.

And the tinker barn—that had been the province of Jim Bishop. He'd taken over the whole of the downstairs and built workbenches and cupboards and what-have-you all along the walls on either side. There were still parts and supplies tucked away in most of the cabinets, although they'd gotten rid of the chemicals for safety after his father had died. No one else knew how to handle the materials.

Shane stood and breathed in the space. He could see his father standing at the workbench, clear as day, wiping down his tools.

"Tell me, son," his dad would say as he looked him over, "two things you learned today. One good and one bad. How about that? Or one small and one large? One meaningful and one insignificant. Your choice."

Shane snorted now, just as he'd done at his dad back then. His dad didn't sound like any other ranch-owning father around. He'd been born and raised on the Bishop ranch, but somehow, his dad had never been meant for it. He'd lived and breathed for books and knowledge, and he wanted his sons to soak it up in the same way he had.

"Hey."

Shane jumped at Cade's voice behind him. The man was silent, he'd give him that. "Shit, Cade, make a little noise next time."

Cade stomped his feet a few times.

"Wise ass."

"Always."

Shane shook his head. "Why aren't you home with your wife?" Shane winced as the words came out of his mouth. It was a good thing Cade knew he didn't have any feelings for Laura that went past sisterly. He'd sounded entirely too bitter.

Cade never was one to rile easily. He leaned against the barn wall, hands in his pockets. "I've got a sick mare. Just checking on her before I head back to the house."

Shane grunted a response. Cade knew where he belonged in the world. With his wife, his family, and his animals.

Shane kept his gaze on the workbench, as though his old man was still standing there waiting for him to name two of the lessons he'd learned that day. You got bonus points if your lessons weren't of the variety taught in school. Cade had been better at those lessons than Shane. Shane had always named something he'd learned in math or science class.

"You think he ever even knew how much she worried about things all the time? How hard it was for her to feed us or put clothes or shoes on us when he spent the whole month's budget on a new experiment?"

Cade hadn't ever resented their dad to quite the magnitude Shane had but he understood Shane's feelings.

"No. I don't think she wanted him to see. Ma was always good at making sure he only saw her support, her love. It's why they worked so well together. She was happiest when she was taking care of us, and that included him. She never would have let him see the strain."

"She should have."

Cade shrugged. "Maybe. Maybe not. We wouldn't have the money we've used to help all these people all these years if she hadn't supported his dreams. If he hadn't done things his way, we might be subject to the same ups and downs all the ranchers around here go through. Who knows if we'd even own the land anymore."

They'd seen a lot of ranchers lose their land or have to sell off parcels in recent years. Others had turned to other ventures, like tourism ranching or raising goats for goat milk soaps.

The ghostly image in Shane's head flickered then came back into form. "Come on, you can think of another one, can't you son? Surely there are two lessons you learned somewhere, from someone you met or talked to along the way today? It's all about the journey, you know. The journey is what you'll have to look back on at the end of your life. Where will your journey say you've been?"

Shane had forgotten the talks his dad had always made time for after school. As much as they'd felt like an inquisition at the time, he could see them for what they were now. His dad had cared. And he'd made the time to make sure Shane knew that, even if it was in his own way.

"What's going on, Shane?" Cade asked.

Shane made a dismissive face. "Nothing. Just thinking back." He looked up at the ceiling above them. Their dad had added a loft to the barn when they were teens. It had padded walls and punching bags. The boys had put in a small kitchenette a few years later. It was where their parents had sent them when they needed to blow off steam. Cade still used it.

Shane searched the ceiling as though it might provide a change of topic for him. "If Laura's brother is..." he stopped, then started back up again. "When we get him out of there, he'll need someplace to go. Someplace he can heal."

He didn't say what he'd need to heal from. In the time since they'd discovered James might be alive, they'd all likely imagined the horrors he might be going through. "We should get some of the guys together and gut the upstairs. We can put in a real kitchen, finish out the walls and insulate it. Turn it into a studio apartment."

Cade looked surprised, then nodded his head. He gestured toward the corner that stood beneath the location of the kitchenette on the second floor. "We could put a bathroom in down here for him. I can see if the Hart brothers would put in a few weekends for us."

The Hart brothers had bought up a few properties in town last year when May Bishop had nudged them in that direction. The four of them had been at loose ends, wreaking all the havoc they could, for as long as they could manage. May had helped give them some direction. She'd also funded their initial purchases. It was one of the projects in town where she'd gone straight to the person and offered money rather than setting up an anonymous grant.

The brothers would do anything May needed of them, and more, without question.

"Not a bad idea," Shane said.

"Just don't mention anything to Laura yet. She's too terrified to hope."

"I don't blame her." He looked over at Cade, throwing a glare in his direction. "And, really, give me more credit. I've got a little more sense than that with women."

Cade let out a snort, not remotely trying to hide it. "Please. If you had more sense with women, you wouldn't be out here in the middle of the night."

"What makes you think this has anything to do with a woman?"

Cade laughed, waving at Shane to follow him as he headed for the staircase against the west wall that led to the loft.

They settled in at the small counter at the kitchenette and Cade pulled two beers from the mini-fridge.

"Laura said you finally asked Phoebe out, that everything was all good."

It didn't surprise Shane that Cade knew his business. This was Evers. Everyone knew everyone's business. It probably hadn't gotten around town yet that she'd dumped him before things had ever gotten the chance to go anywhere, but give it another day. Or another hour.

"Yeah, well, I took her out twice and she ended things. I guess she didn't have a good time."

Cade flinched. "Ouch. I'm sorry."

Shane shrugged. He should have known things wouldn't work with Phoebe. He was made for the Sweater Set ladies.

Boring. Responsible. Jesus, he practically put himself to sleep just thinking about his life.

Phoebe was used to dating guys who rode bikes and got tattoos and knew how to be spontaneous. What the hell would she want with a guy who used spread sheets and pie charts for all major life choices?

37

Dear God, there are days I find your sense of humor lacking.

— FIONA O'MALLEY'S JOURNAL

Phoebe opened her apartment door and hung her purse on the closet doorknob, balancing a bag of left-overs from her dinner. She shuffled through the mail and went to the kitchen to set the bills on the counter and toss the junk into recycling.

"Oh." Phoebe sighed. The refrigerator was filled with leftover take out containers. She really needed to be better about bringing those for her lunch at work. It was ridiculous to be wasting so much food, never mind so much of her paycheck.

She shuffled a few of the containers, set two of the older ones into the sink to rinse and recycle later, and put the new package on the middle shelf.

She'd gone for drinks with Katelyn and Ashley after

work. Drinks had turned into dinner, but then they'd started talking about Fiona's death. The medical examiner's findings and the fact Garret had questioned Elliot was all over town. Phoebe realized she had Fiona's journal and hadn't even thought to give it to the police when Shane first told her about the possibility of the suicide being staged. She'd never looked at the dates at the end of the journal, but with the way it spanned so many years, she wouldn't be surprised if there were recent entries in it.

She walked to the bedroom to grab the book. Ashley had said Garret would be working all night tonight if Phoebe wanted to call and have him pick the journal up. She thought she might take it over to him, instead, though. It was early still, and she didn't mind bringing it by.

Phoebe stopped and stared at the space on her bedside table where the journal had been that morning. The journal was gone.

She looked through the rumpled comforter on her bed. Even in the dead of summer, she slept with a thick comforter over her top sheet. By the morning, she'd always kicked it into a ball at the foot of the bed, but she liked going to sleep with it.

When the journal didn't fall from any of the folds, she bent and pulled up the bed skirt to look under the bed. With one hand, she swept beneath it, wondering how much dust she was disturbing with her search.

A floorboard creaked behind her, and the race of adrenaline hit her body before she had even processed that she'd heard the sound. There was nothing more than a blur in her peripheral vision before the blow came. Phoebe flew forward, reeling.

She put her hand to her head and began to roll, ready to ward off the blow and fight back, but she stumbled forward, the world pitching.

One hand reached for the bedside table as she was thrown forward by the force of another blow, her head striking the table instead of steadying herself on it.

Nausea swept her as the world faded to darkness.

38

With love comes the realization you would gladly give your life for another.

— FIONA O'MALLEY'S JOURNAL

S hane stopped at the intersection between his house and Phoebe's apartment. If he turned left, he could be at her place in just a few blocks. If he turned right, he'd be home in about the same distance.

Home and alone, wishing he were with her. Wishing he'd tried harder.

He gripped the steering wheel and turned left.

What the hell had he been thinking? He'd let her walk away from him without even putting up a fight. He'd let her think he didn't believe she was worth fighting for. Let her think he was willing to walk away without knowing why. Without telling her how much he thought they had a shot at something real.

Maybe she wouldn't care. Maybe she wasn't feeling what he was. But he at least had to try.

His first glimpse of the flames didn't come until he was halfway up her driveway, and at first, he thought he was imagining it.

He wasn't.

Smoke poured from the bottom of her door and flames licked up the window of her living room.

Shane broke into a run and took the stairs in a few leaps that should have left him with a broken neck.

He let out a string of curses as the metal of her doorknob burned his hand. Her door was too damned hot.

Shane flew back down the stairs and pulled his cell phone from his pocket.

"Nine-one-one, what's your emergency?"

He wasn't sure he was entirely coherent but he reported the fire, gave her address and dropped the phone, breaking into a run around the back of the building.

The back of the apartment held a narrow set of stairs leading to a small back porch and door. Shane began to hear the sounds of neighbors coming out and shouts from the street. He blocked all of it out.

He grabbed a rock as he hit the stairs, then tore off his shirt when he reached the top. He moved to throw the rock through the window, but saw the glass was already broken. Worse, several windows along the back length of the apartment had been opened. Someone had been feeding this fire.

He wrapped the shirt around his arm and hand, then reached through the window, opening the door from the inside.

"Phoebe!" Shane raised an arm to block the smoke and heat. He had entered through the kitchen. It wasn't on fire yet, but there was enough smoke to tell him this fire was spreading fast.

"Phoebe! Phoebe!"

Shane probably should have given up when he saw the flames. They were focused mostly in front of her bedroom door. The curtains in front of the living room windows had gone up.

Shane grabbed a blanket from the couch and put it over his head and body. He cursed and took it off, running back to the kitchen for a broom. He didn't know what was piled in front of her bedroom door, but it was engulfed and going up fast. He batted at it with the broom, feeling the flames leap at him, licking the skin of his hands and arms as he pushed the pile of material aside. He tossed the broom and donned the blanket again before kicking her bedroom door in.

The blanket caught fire and he was forced to throw it back out into the living room as soon as he made it through to her bedroom. There would be no using that to get back through the apartment.

Shane found Phoebe unconscious beside the bed.

"Phoebe! Phoebe! Can you hear me?" The sound and heat of the fire was overwhelming. The noise was something he would never forget as he lifted Phoebe and brought her to the window. He talked to her the whole time, as he set her down next to open the window.

She didn't respond, didn't move.

Shane's heart flew in wild, erratic jumps as he saw fire-fighters coming around the corner of the house.

"Here! Over here!" He called out, then pulled Phoebe up, leaning her against the window frame so they could get her first. He didn't know how long she'd been in there breathing in the smoke. He knew enough about fire to know that it was often the smoke that killed people.

Minutes later, he watched as they fed Phoebe oxygen and loaded her into an ambulance. Someone pressed an oxygen mask to his face. Another pair of hands pulled him to sit.

He wrenched away. "I need to go with her." His voice was horse and he knew on some level, he needed to let them treat him. A cough wracked his body, but one voice cut through.

"Shane! Sit. Let them work on you."

Shane looked up to see Garret giving the order. As Shane laid back on the gurney they had been pushing him onto, he met Garret's eyes. "The back door—window was broken. And the windows along the back side of the house were open."

Garret gave a curt nod. "I've got to let the firefighters do their work, but I'll get in there as soon as they have the fire under control. I'll see if we can get an arson investigator sent in from Branson Falls."

Shane laid back. They were loading him into an ambulance now, and he was fine with that. They could drive him to the hospital. When he got there, he was finding Phoebe and he wasn't leaving her side.

39

I've learned, it's always worth keeping your mouth shut until you're sure you can control what's going to come out.

— FIONA O'MALLEY'S JOURNAL

S hane was as patient as he could be with his mother, Cade, and Laura when they got to the hospital. He'd suffered minor burns on his hands and he'd been given oxygen, but he hadn't been able to find out a damned thing about Phoebe. His head was pounding and he wanted to run through the hallways throwing open every door until he found Phoebe.

"Enough!" The nurse jumped at his outburst, and his mother scowled at him, before apologizing for his rudeness.

Shane focused on Cade. His brother would get it. "I need to find Phoebe. I need to see her."

Cade nodded. "I'll find out what I can. Give me a

minute." His hand on Shane's shoulder squeezed, letting him know he'd understood.

Shane looked down at his wrapped hands. "Laura, I need you to look up the number for the Pentagon. Call and ask for a man named Carson and tell them it's an emergency. If they won't put you through, I need somebody to go to my office and find Phoebe's emergency contact information instead."

Laura nodded and picked up her phone, stepping out into the hallway.

His mother's boyfriend, Josh, walked in then. "I've talked to the doctors," he said, and Shane could have kicked himself. Josh had been an emergency room physician for years before he retired and moved to the ranch. Of course, he'd have gone right to the doctors to see what they would tell him.

Josh continued. "They've got two primary concerns right now. Brain contusion and damage to her esophagus and lungs from smoke inhalation. They've intubated her to be sure she maintains an open airway and they've got her headed in for a brain scan. Brain contusions can be self-healing. They won't know the extent of the damage from the smoke for another twenty-four to thirty-six hours. They'll likely keep her sedated for now."

Shane liked that Josh never seemed to use terms that people couldn't understand. He guessed it came from talking to family members in the emergency room. Wherever he'd honed the skill, Shane was grateful for it now. "I need to see her."

Josh nodded. "And you will, but first you need to let them clear you."

Shane was ready to argue, but Josh put a hand on his shoulder. "You need to let them clear you. If you collapse while you're trying to tear-ass through this place looking for her, you're no good to her. Not to mention, no one's going to let you into the MRI theater anyway and that's where she is for the foreseeable future."

Laura walked back in, handing Shane the phone. "I got through. Carson is getting the General."

Shane put the phone to his ear and waited. It was several minutes before General Brophy came on the line.

"Shane? What's happened?"

"Sir," Shane said, feeling the weight of the news he was about to deliver all over again, and suddenly he was the one needing to reassure someone. "There's been a fire. We're at the hospital now and they're running tests and treating her for smoke inhalation."

He stopped when he realized there wasn't any more he could say. He couldn't say she'd be all right, because he didn't know. He couldn't say she wasn't going to suffer long term injuries or even that she wasn't going to die, because he didn't know. He'd never felt so utterly helpless in his life. It turned out, he sucked with helpless.

The General seemed to know Shane couldn't offer him much more. "I'm on my way. Give Carson the details and I'll get there."

Shane gave Carson the name and address of the hospital before hanging up. Now, he had to wait.

40

When love comes, hold it fiercely to you.

— Fiona O'Malley's Journal

S hane sucked at waiting. He would have always said he was a patient man. As it turned out, he was dead wrong. Or maybe he was only impatient when it came to Phoebe and her safety.

He paced the waiting room they'd finally showed them to when they decided he wasn't going to need to be admitted. His family lined the chairs. They'd long ago given up on trying to get him to sit down.

They still occasionally offered food, but his stomach rebelled at even the suggestion.

"Shane."

Shane spun, looking at the small nurse who stood in the doorway. He'd gone to school with her. Samantha or Stacey or something. She had moved to one of the neighboring towns their freshman year, so she wasn't someone he knew well.

He crossed the room in two strides and she sent him a sympathetic smile. His heart clenched as he realized maybe she was here to break bad news. Surely, they would have sent a doctor to do that?

She must have seen the look on his face. She brightened. "She's okay, Shane. They're bringing her up to a room right now. She'll be on the third floor. Head up there and ask at the nurse's station at the west end of the ward. They'll be able to tell you which room."

"She's okay?" His voice was still scratchy from the fire, but he wasn't sure some of it wasn't also from the raw emotion flooding him.

"She is. She's going to need to stay in the hospital for a while so she can have nebulizer treatments and they can monitor her lungs. She might also be in some pain. There might be scarring to her face, but it's also possible the burns might heal without that. They aren't severe."

Shane thought his knees might just give out from the relief. He didn't care about scarring or any of that. He cared that she would live.

His mom came up next to him, and somehow when she looped her arm through his, he'd swear the small woman might be holding him up.

When he saw Phoebe being wheeled into her room on a bed ten minutes later, he finally sucked in the breath that had been eluding him since he'd seen those flames hours before.

Her hair was singed and there were blisters on her face

and places where the skin was peeling and sooty, but the breathing tube had been removed. The nurse looked at him. "We'll get her cleaned up and settled in."

There was an IV in her arm and the nurse set about moving tubes and stands into place. "She's getting pain medication through this. She's pretty out of it. It's got a sedating effect, so don't expect much, but you can talk to her."

He didn't need to be told twice. His eyes had locked onto Phoebe's eyes and he wasn't going to look away. She grinned at him and started to laugh, that gorgeous smile that made him feel nothing but pure joy.

Her laughter turned to a hacking cough, but when she recovered, she spoke. "I might be late for work tomorrow." This was said in a loud whisper and she laughed at her own joke, making his heart clench.

"I'll talk to your boss for you." He wasn't surprised to find his cheeks were wet. She'd scared the ever-loving hell out of him.

He lifted the hand that wasn't filled with tubes and squeezed. "I called your dad, sweetheart. He's coming. Carson texted and said he caught a flight and should be here in a few hours."

"You called me sweetheart." Her eyes were big and round and he couldn't tell if she was bothered by the name or not.

"I did. I'm rejecting your break-up until we've had time to talk about it."

She scowled, scrunching her face at him. "You can't do that. The Junes told me you date everyone and you never commit. I don't want to date another playboy. I've had all the playboys I can handle. If I wanted another playboy, I could go get Ray back."

"The hell you could," he growled.

Her lids lowered. "That's a little sexy when you do that."

The nurse snorted, but Shane shot her a glare and she slipped from the room.

Shane pulled a chair close to the bed and sat, then brought her hand to his mouth and kissed it. "I need you to forget anything the Junes told you until we've had a chance to talk."

"Mindy said it, too," she slurred.

Shane was torn between cursing and grinning. "Forget that, too. We'll talk after you've had a chance to rest. For now, close your eyes."

Her hand tightened on his and her eyes shot open. "Stay!"

"Yes, ma'am," he said, and he did laugh at that, because he felt for all the world like one of Cade's trained dogs. He didn't care. He'd be her trained anything. He just wanted her safe and by his side.

"You won't leave me?"

"Not going anywhere, sweetheart." He ran his hand up her arm. He wanted to reach out and touch her face, let her know he was here, but he was afraid he'd hurt her. "I'm not going anywhere."

41

Let us put our minds together and see what life we can make for our children.

Irish Proverb recorded in Fiona O'Malley's Journal

Unfortunately, the General arrived at about the same time Garret came in with news on how the fire had started. General Brophy wore the mask Shane imagined he wore when headed into battle or, as most of his battles likely took place in strategy rooms nowadays, a meeting. His expression was fierce, unyielding, and it had to be said, downright frightening.

Shane had been telling General Brophy what the doctors had told him when Garret entered the room. After introductions, the three men stepped into the hallway. Shane stayed in front of the door, so he could hear Phoebe if she woke up. He didn't want her waking up alone.

"Your gut was right, Shane," Garret began, "the fire was set."

"The doctors said she had two injuries to her head," Shane told Garret. "I don't think those were an accident, either."

There was a slight pale sheen to the General now and Shane understood it. It reminded him of the sick feeling he'd had since seeing those flames.

"The fire was started right outside Phoebe's bedroom door." Garret paused and looked to the General. "Phoebe was unconscious in her bedroom when Shane found her."

The General shot a look to Shane but nodded to Garret to continue. "There were pillows we believe came from Phoebe's bed piled outside the bedroom door. They were doused in two substances: acetone and cooking oil."

"That doesn't happen by mistake," Shane said, stating the obvious.

"No," Garret said, "it doesn't. I was lucky. I got one of the arson guys to come in right away from Branson Falls. He's headed back now because he's knee deep in another investigation, but he said if he had to guess, whoever did this did some research ahead of time. The acetone was the combustible and the oil was the accelerant. The combination ensured the fire caught quickly and spread fast. It's also a combination of items many people might have in their home. Arsonists try to make use of either items that wouldn't draw suspicion if someone was carrying them in small amounts, or items they can find in the target location."

"Was it a random attack?" The General looked between Shane and Garret, and Shane could see the man didn't think the answer to his question was yes.

Shane shook his head. "I don't know. The law office was

broken into recently. Nothing was taken, but it was clear someone was looking for something."

Garret looked to Shane. "Would anyone have reason to think Phoebe had taken files home with her? Did she, for that matter? Ever take work home with her?"

Understanding dawned on Shane swiftly and it was all he could do not to hit his head on the wall. "Oh hell, Garret. She had Fiona's Journal. I'd completely forgotten about it."

"Fiona is the woman who committed suicide recently?" The General asked.

It was Shane who answered after Garret got a description of the journal and then stepped away to tell his officer on the scene to search for it in Phoebe's apartment. "Up until a few days ago, we thought she'd committed suicide. Now, there's evidence it might have been murder. Phoebe had her journal at her house. I should have remembered she had it as soon as Garret discovered her death might not be a suicide." He looked back to Phoebe's room, his chest tight and feeling like it might crack open. He could have gotten her killed.

"Shane," General Brophy said, one hand on Shane's shoulder and his voice as soft as Shane had heard it when the big man spoke to his daughter. "You saved her life. I don't think I have all the details yet, but that much is clear. I owe you a debt I can't ever repay." The man paused. "She's everything to me."

Shane was beginning to understand the feeling.

I've always wanted my daughter to be stronger than I am. I want her to know love, know her own mind, and, above all, know joy.

— Fiona O'Malley's Journal

"No, dad. I'm not leaving. I'll stay with friends and I'll take precautions, but I'm not going to run." Phoebe sat propped up in bed. She was hoping another coughing fit didn't come on. It wouldn't help her cause. The nurse was due with another nebulizer soon. She would feel better after that.

They'd taken the breathing tube out, and she was told her head was healing, though her headaches were still there.

"It might not be a bad idea, Phoebe. Just temporarily."

Phoebe's jaw dropped at Shane's words. She didn't know

what had happened while she'd been hopped up on pain meds, but her father and Shane were awfully chummy. Well, maybe not chummy, but at least in agreement where orchestrating her life was concerned.

"I know you mean well," she said as she divided a look between the two of them, "but I'm not going anywhere. I'll be careful. I promise."

Shane crossed his arms and Phoebe laughed. "I grew up with him," she said, tossing her head toward her dad. "Do you really think that's going to work on me?"

"She's not going to give in." This came from her father and she almost felt bad for the two of them. They looked so dejected.

"Fine. Stay with me," Shane said. "We'll go to and from work together and I'll take you anywhere else you need to go until this person is caught."

Phoebe was surprised to see her dad nodding his agreement. He wanted her to go stay with Shane? What planet was she on? This was the man who'd once told her prom date he had wired Phoebe's body with sensors and would know if the boy laid a single hand under her dress.

"I can't...I'm not going to..." She stopped. How could she remind Shane they'd broken up if she didn't want her dad to hear the conversation?

Shane raised a brow. "Yes?"

Phoebe pressed her lips together.

"Good. It's settled." Her father crossed his arms now with a nod and Phoebe was left staring at the two men, both in identical poses. Both fully satisfied they'd just MacGyvered the problem brilliantly.

Phoebe sighed. "Fine."

Shane was all grins, but as he sat next to her and took her hand, his face grew serious. "Now, I want to talk to you about something."

Phoebe nodded.

"You and I knew you had the journal," he began. "Margaret, too. Who else knew about it?" His voice was soft and gentle and she had a feeling he was trying not to give her a panic attack.

Phoebe closed her eyes, thinking. "Katelyn and Ashley. I think Laura?" She opened her eyes and looked to her dad. "My dad."

"She told me at the diner," the General said to Shane. "It didn't seem like it was a big secret. Any number of people could have overheard."

Phoebe's eyes flew to Shane's. "Aengus O'Malley was behind us. I saw him come in and sit down, but then forgot he was there."

Shane nodded. "Anyone else you remember seeing there? Or anyplace else you talked about it that someone could have overheard?"

"Not that I can think of. Margaret mentioned that she told Bev one day. She said Bev was worried about Fiona's daughter still not forgiving her mother, so Margaret told her I was searching the journal for a way to help Emmaline."

Shane nodded, face grim. "I'll call Garret and give him the names of everyone you can remember, but keep thinking about it."

The squeeze he gave her hand when he walked away probably shouldn't have made her stomach flutter as much as it did. Phoebe watched him go and tried to come to grips with the hope that was so swiftly building in her heart.

43

There is no need like the lack of a friend.

— IRISH PROVERB RECORDED IN FIONA O'MALLEY'S
JOURNAL

I t wasn't lost on Shane that Phoebe's dad was the exact opposite of his own. General Brophy *was* responsibility. Well, as much as any one man could embody responsibility, anyway.

Shane respected the hell out of him. As far as he could tell, the man was devoted to country and service, but he was equally devoted to his daughter. Phoebe's dad had raised her from her first month of life on, and he never seemed to regret a moment of it.

Oddly, he also reminded Shane of his own dad in some ways. He seemed genuinely interested in everything Phoebe had to say to him. Watching them as they ate dinner at

Shane's place two days later, he realized his own father had always been interested in listening to what he had to say.

All those questions his old man had asked him about lessons learned throughout his day had been because his dad wanted something deeper than "how was your day?"

Shane looked at Phoebe as she grinned a devilish grin at her dad. She was teasing him, and it brought out this playful side of her Shane loved. She looked lovely. She would say otherwise. The whole left side of her hair had been singed and would have to be cut short. For now, she had it wrapped in a scarf. She'd told Shane she planned to go into town in a few days when she was feeling better to have one of the girls at the salon fix it for her.

Her skin was blistered and peeling, with places that were red with the look of skin that needed many months to heal. Because of that, she was scrubbed free of makeup. He loved her that way.

Shane's landline rang and he stepped away to answer it. He spent several minutes on the phone before stepping back into the dining room to find two expectant faces looking at him.

"That was Garret," he said, still a little stunned. "They've arrested Aengus O'Malley for murder."

Phoebe covered her mouth with her hand, holding in a gasp, but it was the General who answered. "He's the ex-husband?"

"Yes," Shane said. "They've had him on their radar, but when you said he might have overheard your conversation in the diner, they looked harder. Apparently, he didn't have an alibi for the time of Fiona's death or for the attack on you.

Garret has spent the last few days tracking down leads and re-interviewing everyone on the block. Someone down the street thought they saw someone matching Aengus's description about an hour before Fiona died, but no one on our block saw his car that day. It turns out, Aengus had parked two blocks over and walked."

"What? He was there? How do they know where he parked?" Phoebe never did have the patience to let a good story come out at its own pace.

"Garret expanded his search and found neighbors who reported seeing the car. And," he smiled now, shaking his head, "the idiot got a ticket. Garret's officer just hadn't put two-and-two together, but the ticket was on file."

"Why did he do it?" Phoebe asked, her eyes filling.

"He claims to have done it for his daughter. Apparently, when Fiona sold her house to Elliot last year, Aengus became suspicious. This year, Fiona gave Elliot power-of-attorney and severely limited her own ability to withdraw funds from her accounts."

The General frowned. "Elliot is the younger boyfriend? Why would she do that?"

"Because she was experiencing signs of dementia. A lot of confusion, swings in her emotions, large chunks of time missing from her memory. She had discovered she'd made several large cash withdrawals from the bank. She said she knew one of them went to the senior center, but she wasn't sure what she'd done with the rest or why she didn't have any records of them."

"So, it sounds like she was addressing the issue. Why did

Aengus…" Phoebe didn't finish, as though she couldn't bring herself to say it.

"Because he didn't trust Elliot. We had set up a trust that made sure money and property that Fiona didn't need during her lifetime went to Emmaline and her kids, but he didn't trust that Elliot wouldn't spend all of her money before that could happen."

"Oh, that's awful." Phoebe shook her head.

"How did he get her to take a fatal amount of her blood pressure medicine?" General Brophy asked.

"It wasn't her medication, actually. That's how they got him to confess. That and the location of the car. When they got a warrant to search his house, they discovered he had a propranolol prescription as well. He was prescribed it for migraines, not for blood pressure, so his dosage was different than Fiona's. When they searched the house, her pills were in his prescription bottle. He crushed his propranolol ahead of time and took it to Fiona's house. It wasn't uncommon for them to have a meal together. Even when they were arguing, they'd remained close. He made her tea and a snack, putting a small amount of the medication into each of the items. Then he took her medication home to use in place of what he'd given her from his bottle. He hoped suspicion would fall on Elliot since he was a pharmacist and would know the danger of propranolol causing shock and cardiac arrest."

"With her gone, everything she had left went to Emmaline?" the General asked.

"Yes. Except the house, which she'd already sold."

"There are still a few things that don't add up," Shane

said. "Garret found trace evidence of Rohypnol on the outside of Fiona's prescription bottle. Aengus claims he knows nothing about that. He's admitted to everything else, though. To breaking into the law office, to attacking you and starting the fire to cover his tracks."

"That's strange," the General said with a frown.

"I agree," Shane said. "Garret is going to ask the medical examiner to run the test again. In the meantime, they've got Aengus on murder one because of the premeditated nature of the crime."

They had to say goodbye to the General soon after. There were things happening at his post that only he could handle. Phoebe ran back in the house to get something for her father, leaving Shane and General Brophy standing on the sidewalk near the car that would take him to the airport.

"I hate that I have to leave her. The job takes me away from her more than I'd like."

Shane looked over, startled at the confession, but found the General staring at the house as though he could see Phoebe inside. Phoebe had told Shane her dad had often been deployed when she was young, and she'd been left with her grandmother to raise her. Never once had Phoebe made it sound like she didn't understand and respect the job her father did.

Shane wanted to say something. Wanted to tell him how much Phoebe loved him, how she thought he was a great dad. That as far as she was concerned, her dad never let her down. Hell, he wanted to tell the man *he* thought he was the perfect dad. That even Shane could see the General was always there for Phoebe when she needed him, even if he wasn't always able to come in person.

He didn't know how to form the words, how to say that, but he didn't have to. The General turned and shrugged. "I have a feeling all fathers think they haven't done good enough by their kids. It's never enough for someone you love," he said.

Shane wondered if his father had thought that, and for the first time ever, he wished he could reassure his dad. All this time, he'd thought his dad wasn't responsible enough for them, that he'd put his inventions and his ideas ahead of the family, and there were times that was true. But looking back, Shane could see his father had loved him unconditionally. When Shane had messed up or made mistakes, his dad had been the one there to talk to him, to tell him it was all right to screw up now and again if you made it right and learned from it.

He'd always thought his dad's role in making him who he was today had been in motivating him to be better than his dad was. Now, he could acknowledge his dad had helped him be who he was today in so many more ways. He'd just been too angry to give the man the credit he was due.

Phoebe's bright smile hit him as she stepped back out of the house, a bag in her hand. "I packed you some snacks, Dad," she said and Shane watched as the giant bear of a man pulled Phoebe in for a hug and a kiss.

Then the General turned to Shane and offered a hand. "Take good care of her for me."

Shane swallowed as he returned the shake.

"Aw, look at you two, having a moment." Phoebe

pretended to wipe tears from her cheeks and sniff. "It's so moving."

"Wiseass," the General said as he pulled her into a hug one more time.

When he was gone, Shane walked with Phoebe into the house, taking her by the hand and pulling her onto the couch with him. He wanted to make love to her. To kiss every inch of her body and see that she was really okay. He wouldn't do any of that. She needed to rest and he would let her, but they did need to talk.

And, he was finding, he needed to touch her, hold her. He needed connection with her right now as though his soul needed the reminder she was here and safe. He stretched on his side on the couch, pulling her back flush to his chest and holding her.

"I think I broke up with you." Her tone was playful, like she'd given up on the idea of breaking up with him.

"Yeah, we need to talk about that. When you were all hopped up on the good stuff at the hospital, you said the Junes told you something. I think I need you to tell me about that conversation."

She went stiff in his arms, and tried to sit up. He didn't let her.

He kept one arm wrapped around her body and put a hand to her hip, steadying her. "Relax. I need to hold you right now." He whispered, his mouth close to her ear. "I almost lost you."

She settled into him and he held her. "Tell me about the Junes. What did they do?"

She shook her head. "I don't think they meant to be

cruel. In fact, I don't think they even realized the effect of their words. They just told me you've dated all of them—both Junes and Mindy—and they had each hoped for commitment, but that you're not that kind of guy." She turned to look at him. "The thing is, Shane, I *am* that kind of girl. I want marriage and a family, and all that. I don't want a quick fling. I'm sorry."

"I don't want that."

Her face fell and she looked wrecked. "I know. It's why we can't do that."

"No," Shane said, bringing his hands up to gently cup her face. "I don't want a quick fling. I'm not interested in that. The reason none of the Junes or Mindy got a commitment was because they weren't the right person for me. All this time, I've been searching for the right woman, but she wasn't here. She was off working in a tattoo parlor and hanging out with shelter animals and putting eyelashes on her car."

She looked stunned for a minute, before that smile he loved formed. "My car likes to feel pretty."

The bark of laughter that came from Shane was for the car joke, but even more for the relief he felt when he processed her words, her smile. She wasn't arguing that they should break up. He was still smiling when he spoke again. "I'm not willing to let you walk away without fighting for you."

"I guess I can give you a few more dates before I make any decisions."

"Wiseass," he said, echoing her dad's sentiments wholeheartedly. She was. But for now, she was *his* wiseass and he was more than happy with that.

He kissed her, softly, letting his mouth float over hers as she sighed in what he hoped like hell was contentment.

He pulled back when he heard her breath start to hitch. She wasn't ready for this. He tucked her back against his chest and wrapped his arms around her again. "Breathe."

She nodded and he heard her focusing on getting her breath back in control.

They stayed like that for a long time and Shane realized, he probably could have stayed that way forever. He was happy.

He ran his fingertips over the burned hairs sticking out of her scarf. "God, if I'd lost you..." His voice cracked and he buried his face in the soft spot between her neck and shoulder.

Her arms came up around his head to hold him. "Lucky for us, all you lost was my hair."

He laughed again, head still buried in her, soaking in the feel of her, the smell of her. "You're going to look gorgeous with short hair."

"Ha!"

Shane sat up and pulled her with him. "Trust me. Gorgeous." He'd needed the change in topic. His head had started to go back to the fear he'd felt when he found her in that fire. Dragons lay that way, for sure.

She pulled out her phone and started to scroll through to a web browser, then showed him what he guessed were hair style websites judging by the pictures. "I'm going to have to go very short," she said, tugging at her singed hair.

"Gorgeous."

She laughed. "So you've said."

"I'll keep saying it."

She pointed at an image. "I was thinking it might be fun to do something like this."

He looked at the screen and saw a woman with short hair that had been dyed a bright purple.

"I look phenomenal in purple, believe it or not."

"I believe it," he said. She'd look phenomenal bald.

"What do you think?" She turned again in his arms to look at him. She wasn't doing him any favors, wriggling like that. He was hard as a rock as it was. "Too much for the office? I suppose it's not very appropriate for a law firm."

He shook his head. "I couldn't care less. Trust me, this is Evers. You can do purple hair."

Wrinkles formed between her brows. "Wouldn't it be the opposite? I mean, it's a small town. Everyone's all judgy and whatnot."

"True," he said. "But it's my law firm and I don't care. I need to keep my favorite paralegal happy."

"I'm your only paralegal."

"You bet your sweet ass, you are."

44

True joy transforms.

— FIONA O'MALLEY'S JOURNAL

S he didn't go with purple. She cut her curls into a short messy look that somehow managed to tempt Shane more than her long curls ever had. If anyone had asked him a week ago if that was possible, he'd have laughed.

He'd been pretty damned fond of running his hands through those curls. Tangling the strands in his hands when he kissed her, tasted her.

When her curls slipped loose of whatever clips she commissioned to try to hold them in during the day, little strands curling at the nape of her neck or on her cheek had seemed like the ultimate distraction to him. He'd thought they would be the death of him.

But this new short look was turning out to be even worse.

Somehow, she looked all businesslike with this new cut, and he found himself constantly wanting to ruffle her neat little skirts and make her lose control.

"Shane." She was using her no-nonsense, you-should-be-paying-attention-to-me voice. Thank heavens they weren't in the office yet. If they were already in the office, he would have to snap out of it and listen to her. He had a self-imposed policy of never disrespecting her when she was in the office with him. Fantasizing about her sitting on him, riding him, as he undid the buttons of her blouse, would fall in the category of disrespecting that fantastic brain of hers.

But right now, they were getting ready to walk out the door. They didn't have any appointments until the afternoon, and there was nothing to stop them from taking an hour to play.

"You're not listening to me at all, are you?" She had her hand on one hip, challenge on her face.

"Not at all." He shook his head but walked slowly backward to the couch. After sinking into the leather, he crooked a finger at her, beckoning her to him.

She gave him a mock look of shock.

He grinned, spreading his legs wide so she could see what she was doing to him.

Phoebe licked her lips as her gaze went to his crotch and it was all over. "Now, Phoebe." This came out on a growl, but her expression told him she didn't mind one bit. In fact, he knew she'd be just as ready for him as he was for her by the time she made it across the room.

She was in on the game now, having dropped her purse and slipped off her shoes.

She took her time, sauntering to him as one hand lazily flicked the buttons of her shirt apart.

He groaned. His erection straining against his zipper.

"We're going to be late," she whispered in a husky voice as she slid her skirt up her thighs.

Shane groaned again. She was wearing thigh high stockings with garters but she'd gone without panties.

"Phoebe." He slid his hands around her hips and back to her bottom, cupping as he pulled her toward him. He needed this woman. It had struck him more than once that he loved her. He didn't think she was ready to hear the words, yet, but he knew in his heart, he'd fallen in love and was going to do everything in his power to make sure she loved him back someday.

He began by bowing his head and worshiping her breasts. She sank into his lap and ground down on him.

Shane reveled in the feel of her in his arms as he stripped her bare. He had to let go of her long enough to stand and remove his own clothes, but when they came back together, the fit was perfect.

She sank onto him in one slow, teasing motion that brought a moan from both of them. From there, it was all he could do to keep from coming hard and fast. He wouldn't let that happen without taking her with him.

He angled to tease one pebbled nipple into his mouth and she cried out when his teeth grazed the bud. Shane anchored his hands at her hips, urging her on, faster, harder. More. So much more.

"Shane!" Her cry was part pleasure, part plea, and he answered her, pushing into her harder and harder.

And then their cries mingled together as they orgasmed as one, and Shane knew he'd lost his heart to this woman forever.

45

Be brave enough to make amends.

— FIONA O'MALLEY'S JOURNAL

Phoebe spotted Emmaline on the porch as soon as she pulled up. She'd arranged the visit ahead of time, and she was hoping it went well. They hadn't been able to recover the journal. Aengus had burned it after reassuring himself it had nothing in it that could point the finger toward him. Apparently, he and Fiona had had a few fights the week before she died, but she hadn't recorded anything in her journal for months.

But Phoebe knew a lot of what was in it, and the least she could do was tell Emmaline some of what her mother had hoped for her to know.

As she came close, Emmaline stood. Phoebe could see she'd been crying.

"My husband took the kids out to the playground so we

could talk." Emmaline looked around as though seeing the world again for the first time in a little while. "I guess I need to find a way to get things back to normal for them. They've been watching me cry for weeks now."

"It can't be easy." Phoebe didn't blame the woman for her state. Lord knew Phoebe's parents hadn't worked out as a couple, but at least one of them hadn't killed the other. She couldn't imagine trying to deal with that blow.

Emmaline led the way into the house and made them iced tea. "We can go out to the back porch."

They sat on wicker chairs under a lazily spinning ceiling fan as Phoebe told Emmaline what her mother had written about in the journal.

"She loved you. She wanted you to know that, I think. I think she wanted you to understand she didn't leave your father to hurt you or even him. She simply needed to put herself first once she knew you were old enough to handle that."

Emmaline picked at the pillow she held in her lap. "I was so selfish when she left my dad. I was angry and didn't want to see that it was what she needed. I only saw that he was hurting. I'd always thought he loved her and was hurt because of that when she left. Now, I wonder if it wasn't his pride more than anything."

"I don't know. I know she saw him as a friend. She talked a lot about what he was like when she met him in Ireland, how he seemed larger than life. She was taken with him, with the idea of him, with the idea of coming to America and leaving what she saw as her small world."

Emmaline didn't seem to need a response. She needed

someone to listen. "It never dawned on me until recently that my mother was sixteen when she met my dad in Ireland. She was only nineteen when they came here to the United States." She looked at Phoebe. "Can you imagine that? Leaving not only your family but all you know? Leaving the country and starting completely over."

"I can't. I'm used to moving around a lot and there would still be parts of it that were overwhelming, even to me. For someone who had never left the town she'd lived in all her life —" Phoebe shook her head—"it must have been frightening for her."

Emmaline nodded. "It makes sense that she felt she needed to find herself, to let herself be the most important thing for a while. I had started to see that and we were making progress, but then when Elliot came along, I watched my dad get hurt all over again and I just didn't want to listen to her side of things."

Tears started to flow again. "I still can't believe my dad killed her. The worst part is that he did it to protect me, but I didn't need or want her money." She looked at Phoebe now. "I just want the chance to have her back, to make up for all the stupid years I kept all of that distance and anger stewing between us."

Phoebe nodded, tears coming to her eyes again for the woman before her, for Fiona, for Elliot, and even for the life Fiona and Aengus had hoped to have together, but hadn't found.

When Phoebe pulled away half an hour later, she hoped she'd at least helped Emmaline a little. If nothing else, she knew her mom thought of her often and loved her.

Phoebe was early when she pulled back into Evers at the end of the two-hour plus drive. She was supposed to meet a few of the women at Elliot and Fiona's house. Elliot had gone to stay with a friend in Seattle for a few days, and the women told him they would do some cleaning out at the house while he was gone. He planned to keep a lot of Fiona's things. He said he wasn't ready to part with everything, but things like clothing and books could go to charity.

Phoebe expected to look for the key he'd told her was hidden on the front porch, but Miriam's car was already in the drive, so she let herself in the unlocked front door.

"You're early, too, Miriam?" She called out as she entered. She heard noise in the kitchen and moved that way.

The scene startled her. Miriam was up on a stool pulling tins and boxes of tea from the cabinet. That might not be unusual if they intended to clean out all of Fiona's tea, and really, Phoebe wasn't sure they couldn't do that. She supposed Elliot wouldn't want to hold on to Fiona's tea.

But Miriam was in a panic. She was opening boxes and tins, dumping the contents on the counter top. She didn't seem to notice—or maybe it was that she didn't care—that tea bags were falling onto the floor.

"Miriam," Phoebe said, stepping closer. "Is everything all right?"

Miriam spun, with a startled cry. "Oh, Phoebe. Oh, I'm sorry. You startled me."

Phoebe let her gaze travel over the counter and floor. "Is there something I can help you with?"

"Oh, no, no. I just wanted to clean out the teas. They can start to smell bad if you let them expire."

Phoebe frowned and looked again at the mess. She'd let tea go darned good and stale in her cabinets plenty of time. In fact, she kept some for years at times without ever cleaning them out. She'd never once had a problem with them smelling. Tea was already dried when it was made.

"Okay," she said, wondering if there was something she could do to help calm Miriam. Arguing about tea wouldn't help. Miriam had been devastated by the news of Fiona's death and she didn't want to make this harder than it already was for the woman.

Miriam looked at the floor. "Oh, I guess I've made a mess. I can't find some of the tea I made for her. It seems to be missing." She was shaking as she bent to scoop up the teabags.

"I'm sure it's here somewhere," Phoebe said, bending to help and putting a hand over Miriam's with a squeeze. "I'll help you look."

Miriam looked up with a little sigh and offered a small smile. "Oh, no it's fine. I just overreacted when I couldn't find it. I'll just get rid of these ones and then we can see what else needs to be done around here."

Phoebe nodded. "Okay. Why don't I run upstairs and start in the closet? Elliot said there's an organization in Branson Falls that gives clothes to women who are applying for jobs and might not have appropriate clothes. If we get them all organized today, Ashley said she could bring them over there tomorrow."

"That sounds perfect." Miriam looked around the kitchen. "I'll see if there's anything else around here that we might clean out."

"I wonder if Emmaline might like any of her mother's things. I mean, Elliot won't want to get rid of dishes and things he'll use, but if there's anything like maybe..." Phoebe frowned. She had no idea what she was trying to say.

Miriam must have understood where she was headed. "Fiona has some beautiful tea sets. She liked to collect them on her travels with Elliot. I think he'd be happy to have Emmaline have some of them."

"Perfect." Phoebe went upstairs to begin going through the closet. It felt invasive, but she knew Elliot didn't have the heart to do this himself, and something told her Fiona would hate to see her things sitting unused. Shortly afterward, she heard Ashley and Laura come in. They talked to Miriam for a bit and then came upstairs.

"Hey, Miriam thought you could use our help up here," Laura said as she and Ashley walked in the room. "She's downstairs pulling everything out of the cabinets and washing the shelves and things."

Phoebe stopped, a pile of skirts in her arms. "I think she's taking this really hard. I guess if cleaning and scrubbing helps her through this, I'm all for it."

Ashley faked a shiver. "Cleaning never helped me, but if it helps Miriam, more power to her."

The women shared a smile before digging into the clothing piles.

It took another hour with all of them working together, but in the end, they had several boxes packed up. Some would go to the working women charity in Branson Falls and the others would go to the Goodwill in Branson Falls.

Ashley rearranged the closet to spread Elliot's things

onto both sides of the racks. "I hate to think of him coming home to one side completely empty."

Laura and Phoebe stood alongside her, looking into the closet. "I know what you mean. Either way, it's going to hurt to see the change."

Phoebe shook off the sorrow, knowing they needed to keep moving if they were going to make any progress. It would be too easy to sit and think about all the pain Aengus O'Malley had caused, or all the loss Elliot had dealt with in his life. "Hey, Ashley, you should see if there are any books the Friends of the Library might want. Elliot said all the novels in the room down the hall were Fiona's and you were welcome to them for the library book sales."

The three moved down the hall to the small room. It was not as large as a bedroom might be, but it was beautiful. The walls were a light violet, so light it was almost white. There were windows along two sides of the room that looked out on Fiona's garden. A comfortable chair took advantage of the light in that corner and the rest of the room held shelves of books and knitting projects.

Phoebe picked up the knitting and fingered the soft wool. "It's so sad. She was still so young, when you really think about it."

They began looking through books. "We're going to need a lot more boxes for this," Laura said.

Ashley sat back and looked around. "I can run over to the library and grab some. I'm not sure how many we have, but we have a few. I could stop at the liquor store and grab some from there."

"Sounds good." Laura looked out the window. "It's

getting close to dinner time. Do you guys want me to grab a pizza and we can keep going?" She looked at Phoebe. "Unless you want to go grab it. You've been here the longest if you want to take a break."

Phoebe shrugged. "I'm fine here."

The two women left and Phoebe pulled her phone from her pocket to text Shane.

Going to eat pizza here with the girls. Meet you at home in a few hours? She pressed delete and adjusted the question. *Meet you at your house in a few hours?*

She had started to think of his place as her home. No, that wasn't right. She was thinking of it as *their* home, but she wasn't sure if Shane was on the same page as she was. She knew in her heart, she loved him. She wanted to build a life with him more than anything. She just wasn't sure he was ready for that step. Her feelings seemed to have come so quickly. As far as she could tell with her less-than-perfect judgment of men, it took more time for men to feel the same way about a woman.

Minutes later, Shane texted back.

I'm leaving my mom's place in a bit. I can swing by there and help you guys.

Phoebe looked at the piles of books she'd been sorting and hurriedly typed back a *yes, please!* Having Shane to carry the books to the car wouldn't be a bad idea at all.

She began sorting through the books again, setting them in stacks by genre and type to make it easier for the Friends of the Library organization to decide what to do with them. From what Ashley had said, some of them might go right into the library lending collection, but others would be sold in the used book sale the Friends held each year to raise funds for library projects. She looked up at the sound of someone entering the room, realizing she'd lost track of the time.

"Miriam! Are you all finished with the kitchen?"

Miriam nodded, but Phoebe saw her eyes flick to the small table in the corner. It held an electric tea kettle and a few tea cups. There were several little jars of tea as well.

"I'll just get these taken care of," Miriam said as she crossed and lifted the jars of tea. "We don't want bugs coming in here."

Phoebe turned and stood, assessing the other woman. Miriam turned and froze when she realized Phoebe had gotten up. "Miriam, tea doesn't smell when it spoils and it doesn't attract bugs."

Phoebe said this gently. She had thought the woman might be overwrought about her friend's death. That maybe she might need someone to talk to. That she might need a friend to open up to. Phoebe and Miriam weren't close, but if she could help, she'd like to.

A fierce flash of anger and something else crossed Miriam's face. Was it panic?

"I just need to get rid of it." Miriam's words came out harsh and angry.

Phoebe stepped back in surprise.

Miriam pushed past Phoebe, her lips pressed together as though she'd said something she hadn't meant to.

Phoebe watched her go, then shook her head as Miriam's words came through the surprise. Get rid of what?

Phoebe began to move before she really thought things

through. She caught up with Miriam on the stairs and pulled on the woman's arm.

"Get rid of what, Miriam? What's going on?" Questions whirled through her head so fast, she didn't process that Miriam had spun on her.

Miriam screamed, and the sound was guttural, almost inhuman, as she launched at Phoebe. "It wasn't supposed to happen this way. None of it was supposed to happen!"

Miriam dug her nails into the still tender flesh of Phoebe's face and Phoebe cried out. She raised her arms to try to ward off the blow, and maybe to strike back, but her body seemed to be moving in slow motion, like it simply couldn't catch up to what was happening.

Then they were falling, tumbling down the stairs, her screams mixing with Miriam's. Phoebe heard Shane shouting as pain tore through her body. Her head, her back, everything seemed to hurt.

She lay, battling against the pain in her head, feeling sick. But, then Shane was there, his hands running over her. "Are you all right? Talk to me, Phoebe."

"My head."

Gentle hands felt her head. When he got to the back of it, she couldn't stop the cry of agony. White hot pain blinded her.

"Stay still, Phoebe. You're bleeding. I'm calling an ambulance."

"Miriam?" Phoebe couldn't get out more than the one word.

"She's unconscious," Shane said. "What happened?"

"I don't know. She'd been acting strange and then she

said something about destroying something. I tried to talk to her..."

She closed her eyes.

"Open your eyes Phoebe," Shane said as he spoke into the phone telling the nine-one-one operator where they were and that they needed the police and an ambulance.

Phoebe tried to open her eyes, but she was so tired. Her body was beyond tired. She was exhausted. She just needed to rest.

"Phoebe, open those gorgeous eyes, baby. Open up and talk to me."

Processing his words didn't seem to be a problem, but getting her body to actually do anything in response seemed to be impossible. The last words she heard as she slipped away were words of love. Shane Bishop telling her he loved her. That she couldn't leave him.

"I'm sorry, Shane," she wanted to say, but there was no way to make the words come. The exhaustion took over and she gave in.

46

Treasure the people who bring you joy and love. They are, in the end, the most valuable gems you will ever collect.

— FIONA O'MALLEY'S JOURNAL

"I think we're going to have a problem if this becomes a habit. Strike that, it seems to be becoming a habit."

Shane turned at the words of General Brophy behind him.

"Believe me, Sir, I'm as upset as you are about that." He offered his hand and the man took it, but held it firmly as he eyed Shane for a long minute. A very long minute.

"I believe you are," he said as he seemed to come to some kind of decision. "Tell me how it is that they had the murderer in custody when I left here and my little girl is still laying in a hospital bed."

"I'm not sure I can be considered your little girl anymore, daddy. I'm twenty-nine."

Both men turned, each going to one side of the bed.

"Always, my Phoebe." The General looked over at Shane. "Your guy was about to tell me what the hell happened."

A nurse stepped in then, coming to the bed on Shane's side. It killed him to step aside, but he did it long enough to let her check machines and tubes and monitors. She asked some questions and Phoebe answered, sounding better than he'd thought she would with all she'd been through. With her other recent head injury, their main concern had been watching for swelling of the brain, but so far, Phoebe seemed to be acing the questions.

"The doctor's going to be in shortly. We've let him know you're awake." The nurse turned to the men. "Don't wear her out, gentlemen. She needs to rest right now more than anything."

When she'd left the room, Shane went back to Phoebe's side, lifting her hand. He was pretty sure if the doctor walked in right now, he was going to have to fight Shane for access, at this point.

"All right, out with the story." The General grumbled.

Shane looked across at him and started at the beginning since the man didn't know the players like he and Phoebe did. "There's a senior center in town where Fiona spent a lot of time. Do you remember I said Fiona's ex-husband was worried because Fiona seemed to be losing large chunks of money?"

The General gave a single nod and Shane continued. "The center has been run by Miriam Green for the last ten years. Apparently, a few years ago, she realized she was getting closer in age to the center's patrons, and she didn't have any plan in place for someone to take care of her when she hit the age where she would need it. She started to manipulate money out of people a little at a time."

"How did she do that?" Phoebe asked.

"She was using a date rape drug. Rohypnol," Shane said. "She was feeding it to them a little at a time both at the center, and in tea she sent home with them. She would only lace some of the tea bags with it so none of them connected the tea to the onset of symptoms. They'd begin to experience periods of confusion, lapses in memory, mood swings. She would show up and say they told her they planned to donate money to the center and she'd counted on their donations. She managed to convince most of them to give her cash, saying the center had lost its tax-exempt status and they would be helping her out if they paid her cash. She pocketed the cash. She would then show up weeks later saying the same thing; that they'd promised the money and hadn't gotten it to her."

Shane took a deep breath. "It was why she was so upset over Fiona's death. She thought she'd driven Fiona to kill herself. It was the first time one of her targets had died of anything other than natural causes."

"That's horrible," Phoebe said. Shane agreed. The people who went to the center had trusted her. Hell, the whole town had trusted her.

Tears filled Phoebe's eyes. "Poor Fiona. She was targeted by two people. She was such a wonderful person, and yet two people who should have cared for her went after her."

"I have a feeling Miriam's going to spend a lot of years in

prison for her crimes, and Aengus is looking at premeditated murder. They'll pay for their crimes."

"I think I might need you to move back to the big, bad city, Pheebs. This small-town living is going to kill me." The General sank down into a chair, putting a hand over his heart in a mock gesture of defeat.

Phoebe's eyes flew to Shane's and he wondered if she knew that if she was leaving, he was following. There was no way he was staying without her. No way he wouldn't follow her to the ends of the earth.

"Sorry, Dad. I really like it here." She grinned, like she knew the rest of that sentence should have been, "despite the repeated close brushes with death."

Shane leaned close. "I'd follow you, you know."

"You would?" Her eyes went round and soft and she had the look in her eye of a woman who couldn't let herself believe that. "You would follow me?"

Shane heard the door shut and turned to see the General had slipped out. He turned back to Phoebe, pulling his chair closer. "In a heartbeat, Phoebe. I don't plan to let you go."

"You don't?" she asked, still with disbelief threaded through her tone.

Her expression tugged at Shane's heart. "Hell no. I love you, Phoebe Joy. I love you with all my heart, with all that I am."

"You do?"

Shane laughed. "Do they have you on the good meds again and they forgot to tell me?"

47

There are good ships, and there are wood ships, but the best ships are friendships.

— IRISH PROVERB RECORDED IN FIONA O'MALLEY'S
JOURNAL

"Listen, woman," Ashley said as she walked into Phoebe's hospital room an hour later. "If your plan is to keep getting attacked to lure Shane to your side, we have better ways. We can give you a few pointers."

Laura and Katelyn stood by Ashley on either side grinning. Ashley had that effect on people and Phoebe was no exception. She smiled wide.

"When are they letting you bust out of here?" Ashley asked.

"Soon, I hope," Katelyn said with a shiver. "I hate hospitals. They should let you go home to heal. I swear, you'll heal much faster that way."

"They are. Shane and my dad went to grab lunch but by the time they get back, the doctor should have cleared me."

"How did you get those two to leave? I can't imagine it was easy." Laura shrugged apologetically. "What? I can use some tips. Cade is alpha and overbearing, too." She looked at Katelyn and Ashley. "You two could use some ideas, too. She was raised by a general. Surely, she has ideas for us."

Katelyn and Ashley seemed to think on it for a minute before nodding. "Truth," Ashley said.

"I lied." Phoebe blinked at them as though the answer should have been obvious.

All three women were quiet for a minute before Ashley burst out laughing. "About what?"

Phoebe grinned. "I told my dad the nurse was coming in to give me a sponge bath and he should get Shane out of here for a little while. He practically lifted Shane by the collar and hauled him down to the cafeteria."

"Where he only stayed long enough to get you a sandwich, little minx." They all swung to see Shane standing in the door with a take-out container. He walked around the other women and planted a kiss on Phoebe's lips.

"But, how did you get away from my dad?" Phoebe asked.

"We ran into Gina on the way out. She was coming up to see you." Shane visibly shivered. "That woman actually flirted with him." He paused. "In front of me. And he flirted back. You owe me for that one, Phoebe."

Phoebe grinned and whispered up at him. "I'll make it up to you later."

"Oh! That's our cue to leave," Laura said.

The women leaned in for hugs and promises to have lunch as soon as Phoebe was feeling up to it.

When they'd left, Shane opened Phoebe's food for her. "Scoot over," he said, sitting next to her on the bed. He hung off and didn't look at all comfortable, but he handed her the sandwich and acted like there was no place he'd rather be.

Phoebe took a bite. It might come from the hospital cafeteria, but it was better than the food they'd brought to her room. "So, how did you know I wasn't getting a sponge bath?"

"You had your hair in a headband when I left last night."

Phoebe looked up at him and waited, but he looked as if that explanation should have made the answer plain. "And?" She prompted.

"When your hair is in a headband and you take it out, it looks different than it does now. So, I know you showered this morning."

Phoebe wasn't sure what it said about her that her heart did a little flip-flop at that. But somehow, knowing he paid that careful of attention to her sent the butterflies in her stomach flitting about. "Oh," was all she thought to say.

He grinned and dropped a kiss to her mouth. "I pay attention."

He really did, she realized, and she knew he never would have been with her for over a year without knowing what she had wanted, like Michael had. She could see that Michael truly hadn't known she wanted to be married someday. He saw her as the fun girl, the one who just wanted to flit around and have a good time.

Shane knew her in ways other people didn't. He saw her

for who she was, but also for who she could be. He looked at her and saw all the possibilities, and he cheered her on.

He smiled at her. "What are you thinking about?"

"I thought men were supposed to run from that question, not ask it."

He shrugged. "I told you I knew you showered and you seemed to go someplace else for a bit. Can't help but wonder where you went."

"Just thinking that you know me."

He seemed to puzzle on her face for a minute, before his mouth broke out in a smile. "I do." He leaned in and kissed her. "And I love you. Every bit of you."

48

I will hold you in my heart forever, Mom.

— EMMALINE O'MALLEY SHANNON IN A LETTER TO
HER MOTHER, FIONA, WRITTEN AFTER HER MOTHER'S
DEATH

Phoebe knelt and reached into the back of her closet. The studio above the garage still reeked of smoke. There wasn't much that could be salvaged. Mrs. Sasson had decided to tear the structure down rather than rebuild, and Phoebe was fine with that. She was happy at Shane's. But there was one thing she'd wanted to come in and get before the wrecking crew got to work.

She pulled the large box out. The water from the fire-fighters hadn't drenched everything in her closet since most of the flames had been in the other room.

She opened the box and pulled out the two smaller

boxes inside. One held things she'd collected over the years. Notes her dad had sent to her during deployments, pictures and the fan her grandmother had given her when she was little. There were a few pieces of jewelry from her grandmother and the tassel from Phoebe's high school graduation cap. She pulled that one out and set it aside.

The other one, she laid in her lap. She had opened it only a week ago to look at the letters she'd written to her mother, but it seemed like ages had passed since then. She'd only ever sent one letter to her mother. These others, she hadn't ever mailed. She supposed in a way, they were for herself, not for her mother.

They were for a little girl who desperately wanted to hold onto the idea that maybe the woman who gave birth to her would come back one day. That maybe one day she'd realize she'd made a mistake in walking away. That she might want a chance to know Phoebe. To hold her and love her.

Phoebe looked up as Shane entered the room. He scanned the area and she thought she saw him shiver.

"It's hard to come in here. I keep picturing..." he swallowed and didn't finish the sentence. She knew what he meant.

"I have a feeling it's harder for you than it is for me. I was out cold during all of it," she said.

He came and sat next to her. "What have you got there?"

Phoebe opened the box and pulled a letter out, handing it to him. When he had opened it and scanned the contents, he nodded, handing it back. "You said you wrote to her once?"

"Yes. She didn't respond."

"It was only one letter. Do you want to try again?"

Phoebe shook her head. "I might have, but my grandmother found me crying in my room a week or so after I sent the letter. She said she had tried, too. My dad tried throughout the years. I faced facts a long time ago." She turned to look at him. "My mom truly doesn't want anything to do with me."

Shane put one hand to her cheek and caressed, and she leaned into the touch. "I'm so sorry, Phoebe. I wish things could be different with her."

She nodded and looked back at the letters. "I think I'm ready to get rid of these." She closed the lid and ran her hand over the box.

"Are you sure?" Shane's tone said he would be with her either way. He'd support her if she wanted to hold out hope for something more with her mom, no matter how foolish the dream.

She looked at him, and had no doubts, then. "Yeah, I am." She put aside the box and turned so she faced him. "I have everything I need now. I have a home. I have a community. I have friends I value and love. I have my dad. And," She leaned in close, putting her forehead to his as she whispered, "I have you. The hole I had inside me for so long is gone."

His hand came around the back of her neck and she heard him still. He seemed to just be breathing her in, and she was happy to let him do that for as long as he liked. She was happy to sit and breathe him in. To revel in the fact they'd found each other.

She was well and truly whole now.

"I love you, Phoebe Joy." His words filled her with pure bliss and she wanted him to feel the same.

She raised her hands to the sides of his face as she closed her eyes. "I love you, too, Shane Bishop."

EPILOGUE

When you find love, you'll know it. Your doubts and fears will no longer seem significant. They'll be washed away by the sure comfort of knowing there is someone in the world who takes you as you are, who loves you without bounds, and who will be there with you through all the rain life showers upon you.

— Fiona O'Malley's Journal

Three weeks later, Phoebe sat wrapped in Shane's arms after Sunday dinner at his mom's house. Laura and Cade sat on the floor against the couch, a blanket wrapped around them as the credits to the movie played.

Josh and May sat on the other couch, with Jamie May asleep between them.

Laura and Phoebe sighed contentedly at the same time and then began to laugh. They'd been the ones pushing to watch *50 First Dates*.

Both women looked at each other. "There's nothing better than a first kiss," they said in unison, echoing a line from the movie.

It had been weeks since Shane had taken Phoebe home from the hospital that last time, and he never planned to let her go. Life with Phoebe was, simply put, joy. It was everything he'd wanted, and more he couldn't have imagined. He never would have guessed how happy making Phoebe smile could make him. Or how incredible it felt to hear her sigh and whisper his name as she wrapped herself around him in the morning.

Shane leaned in to whisper in her ear. "If I get you home soon, we can relive our first kiss, again and again and again."

Phoebe blushed, just as he hoped she would.

"Love you." He whispered that one close enough that she would feel more than hear the words. She nuzzled into him and smiled.

"I love you, too, Shane Bishop."

They were in their own small cocoon when the world burst back in around them. All heads turned as headlights cut across the night sky outside the window.

"Late for a visitor," Josh said, likely voicing the thoughts of everyone.

They all stood and followed Josh to the kitchen where he pulled open the door before their visitor could knock.

Laura's former mother-in-law, Martha Kensington, stood framed in the doorway wrapped in a sweater, her hair up in a sloppy bun. Shane knew Martha didn't normally leave the house without her hair done and at least lipstick on.

The woman seemed to scan the room, her eyes landing

on Laura. Their eyes locked and Martha swallowed before she spoke. It was then that Shane saw the tremble in the woman's chin. "They've got him, Laura. They've got James."

Shane pulled Phoebe to him and held her, needing the contact as his family took the hit. He heard a choked sob from his sister-in-law and saw Cade wrap strong arms around his wife.

Phoebe had given him more than her heart. Thanks to Phoebe, his sister-in-law would be getting her brother back.

Dear Reader,

I'm so glad you found the Heroes of Evers, TX Series. I hope you love reading them.

Next up is *Cherish and Protect*. This one is James's story and I can't wait for you to read it: loriryanromance.com/book/cherish-and-protect.

Fall in love with all the heroes of Evers in each of their stand alone novels, available now.

Love and Protect

Promise and Protect

Serve and Protect

Honor and Protect

Desire and Protect

Cherish and Protect

Treasure and Protect

Thank you to D.P. Lyle, MD for all of your generous expertise on this book. It's greatly appreciated. Thank you to John and Shari Bartholomew and all of the other people who stopped what they were doing to answer questions for me.

ABOUT THE AUTHOR

Lori Ryan is a NY Times and USA Today bestselling author who writes romantic suspense, contemporary romance, and sports romance. She lives with an extremely understanding husband, three wonderful children, and two mostly-behaved dogs in Austin, Texas. It's a bit of a zoo, but she wouldn't change a thing.

Lori published her first novel in April of 2013 and hasn't looked back since then. She loves to connect with her readers.

For new release info and bonus content, join her newslettter here: loriryanromance.com/lets-keep-touch.

Follow her online:

facebook.com/loriryanromance
twitter.com/Loriryanauthor
instagram.com/loriryanauthor